DOCTOR WHO AND THE MUTANTS

DOCTOR WHO
AND THE MUTANTS

Based on the BBC television serial *The Mutants* by
Bob Baker and Dave Martin by arrangement with the
British Broadcasting Corporation

TERRANCE DICKS

A TARGET BOOK
published by
the Paperback Division of
W. H. ALLEN & Co. Ltd

A Target Book
Published in 1977
by the Paperback Division of
W.H. Allen & Co. Ltd
A Howard & Wyndham Company
44 Hill Street, London W1X 8LB

Reprinted 1979
Reprinted 1982 (twice)

Printed in Great Britain by
Hunt Barnard Printing Ltd, Aylesbury, Bucks

ISBN 0 426 11690 9

Contents

1

The Hunters

It was a planet of jungles. Hot, dense, steamy tropical jungles, filled with a thin, choking mist that drifted eerily between knotted tree-trunks, festooned with dangling vines.

An old man came bursting through the undergrowth. He was thin and wiry, dressed in ragged white robes. His chest was heaving as he sobbed for breath, his staring eyes full of panic as he looked back over his shoulder. From behind him came the crashing of booted feet. He was being hunted.

He could hear voices now as his pursuers came closer. Savage, exultant voices, like the baying of hounds on a scent.

'Over here! Move in this way!'

'The river ... he's heading for the river.'

'After him! Cut him off! Mutt! Mutt! Mutt!'

The voices seemed to come from all around. The old man paused, confused, unsure which way to flee. Then, panicked by the ever-nearing voices, he dashed blindly on. As he ran, his thin sweat-soaked robe clung wetly to his back. His spinal vertebrae were distorted, almost reptilian, running in a row of enormous knobs down his back. Crouching insect-like, the old man staggered on.

He broke through into a clearing, then stumbled to a halt. Someone was standing there, motionless, as if waiting for him. The old man's dazed eyes took in the bulky black-uniformed figure, the cruel, heavy-jowled face with its tiny eyes, and his head bowed in hopeless resignation.

With a smile of savage anticipation, the Marshal of Solos raised his blaster.

Nearby in the jungle, Stubbs and Cotton, the Marshal's aides, bodyguards and general henchmen, heard the shot and exchanged looks of weary disgust. They had served with the Marshal for many years and were used to his brutal ways. But this new passion for hunting down and exterminating the Mutant natives, 'Mutts', as they were called, was getting out of control.

Cotton adjusted the oxy-mask beneath his helmet. 'Mutt mad, he is,' he muttered. 'It's like sport to him.' Cotton was a tall lean man whose ebony features indicated African ancestors back on faraway Earth.

Stubbs, shorter and more thick-set, had spotted something on the trail ahead. 'He's even dropped his mask!'

They heard the Marshal's bellow. 'Stubbs! Cotton! Over here.'

Stubbs picked up the mask. 'Come on—before he passes out.'

They found the Marshal standing triumphantly over the body of the old man. It looked spindly and frail beside his massive bulk. Cotton grimaced under his mask. 'Wonder he doesn't want his picture taken— with his foot on its chest,' he thought. He decided he'd better get a grip on himself. That kind of idea had been popping up rather too much lately—and the Marshal had unpleasant ways of dealing with critics.

Gauntletted hands on hips, the Marshal glared at them. He jabbed the old native's body with his boot. 'Get rid of this disgusting mess. Make out the usual report.' Snatching the face-mask from Cotton, the Marshal strode off, well pleased with his morning's work.

Cotton watched him disappear into the jungle. 'Stinking rotten planet,' he grumbled. 'Can't even breathe properly. Should have given 'em independence years ago.'

Stubbs clapped him on the shoulder. 'Cheer up,

soldier. Not long now.' He took the communicator from his belt. 'Stubbs to Skybase. Marshal's party now returning. Have dealt with Mutant native alert, area seven. Mutant tracked and found dead. Cause of death—unknown.'

The tall white-haired man in the ruffled shirt and elegant velvet smoking-jacket sat hunched over the complex piece of electronic equipment. A very small, very pretty, fair-haired girl sat perched on a lab stool next to him.

The Doctor was working absorbedly, his long fingers manipulating a maze of complex circuits with delicate precision. Jo Grant, his young assistant, looked on rather forlornly. Things were quiet at the British H.Q. of the United Nations Intelligence Taskforce —UNIT for short. For the time being the Earth seemed to be free of attacks from outer space. This meant that the Doctor, currently serving as UNIT's Scientific Adviser, should have had very little to do. However, someone of the Doctor's many interests could always find a way to occupy himself. He'd been working for hours now, and showed no sign of wanting to stop. Jo heaved a sigh, but the Doctor didn't even notice. Reproachfully she said, 'Doctor, are you going to be much longer?'

'Nearly finished, Jo.'

'What are you doing anyway?'

The Doctor looked up. 'I'm making a minimum-inertia Superdrive,' he explained—or rather failed to explain. Jo's blank face made it clear she was none the wiser. The Doctor grinned and went on with his work.

Jo felt a sudden pang. 'For your information, Doctor, it happens to be long past lunch time ...' She broke off. Something was appearing, materialising out of thin air, on the lab bench in front of them. It was a small black box.

The Doctor heard Jo's gasp of astonishment, glanced up, and caught sight of the box. 'Oh dear,' he said. 'Oh dear, oh dear, oh dear!'

Jo looked at the Doctor then back at the box. 'Lunch?' she asked hopefully.

'I'm afraid not, Jo.'

Jo backed away. 'A bomb?'

'Nothing so exciting.'

'Then what is it?'

'An assignment. A little job for me.'

'Then it *is* something exciting!'

The Doctor looked sourly at the little box. 'This thing is a kind of despatch box—from *Them*.'

Jo knew he was referring to the Time Lords, the mysterious, all-powerful rulers of his own race. They had exiled the Doctor to Earth for some unknown offence. The TARDIS, apparently a police box, but in reality a ship that travelled through Space and Time, was no longer working. But this didn't seem to stop the Time Lords using the Doctor as a kind of secret agent.

Jo nodded towards the box. 'Aren't you going to open it?'

'I'm not *supposed* to open it,' said the Doctor crossly. 'Couldn't even if I wanted to. It's only meant for one person, or creature ... and it will only open for one person ...'

'Or creature?'

'That's right. *I'm* just the messenger boy!'

Jo heard the resentment in his voice. 'Why not just refuse? Don't touch the thing.'

'I can't, Jo. The Time Lords' code. They only use this system in a real emergency. It's like a three-line whip in your Parliament. I've *got* to go.'

'Where?'

The TARDIS door swung open of its own accord and a strange wheezing, groaning sound filled the air. The Doctor's face lit up. Jo could see that even in these circumstances he was overjoyed to be on his travels again. 'I think my destination's already been decided,' he said. He grabbed his cloak from a peg and made for the TARDIS.

Jo ran after him. 'I'm coming with you.'

'Out of the question. Bound to be difficult. Probably dangerous too.'

'All the more reason, Doctor. You know you need me to look after you.'

'Sorry, Jo. The answer's no, and that's that!'

The Doctor disappeared inside the TARDIS and the door began closing behind him. Jo sprinted across the laboratory and jumped through the fast-narrowing gap just in time.

Inside the huge, brightly-lit control room of the TARDIS, the Doctor was already checking over the instruments on the many-sided control console. He looked up in some astonishment. 'Jo! Get back in the laboratory at once!'

Jo gave him a cheeky grin and pointed to the glowing transparent column in the centre of the console. It was rising and falling rapidly. 'Too late, Doctor. We're already on our way!'

After what seemed a very long journey, the TARDIS landed. The door opened as mysteriously as before, and Jo and the Doctor stepped outside.

Jo had been expecting something alien and exotic, and her first feeling was one of disappointment. They were in a small, dusty, metal-walled room. It had a round window, a closed door, and that was all. 'Well, where are we?'

'I'm not sure, Jo. But wherever it is, we seem to have arrived at the tradesmen's entrance. Where's the red carpet, eh? What kind of reception is this?'

Jo crossed to the porthole on the other side of the room. 'Doctor, come and look. We're flying!'

The Doctor looked. Far below them in space hung

the mist-shrouded shape of a planet. 'Not exactly flying, Jo. We're in planetary orbit. We must be on some kind of——'

'Skybase One. This is Skybase One,' boomed a smug-sounding metallic voice—as if finishing the Doctor's sentence for him. 'Duty personnel to reception and transfer section. Clear visiting party, escort through bacteriological decontamination.'

The Doctor noticed a speaker grille set high in the wall. 'Well, well, well! Maybe we are expected after all!'

Jo was still trying to make sense of the announcement. 'Escort through bacterio-what?'

'Put less scientifically, Jo—de-lousing.'

'Cheek!' said Jo indignantly.

For once the Doctor was mistaken. The loudspeaker announcement had nothing to do with himself and Jo. As yet no one on Skybase One was aware of their presence. The reception committee in the arrival area was awaiting very different visitors.

It was a strangely mixed party that stood by the line of materialisation cubicles. Dominating the group was Varan. War Chief of Solos, he was a tough-looking figure in his forties. His ceremonial robe left his brown chest bare, and his short, curved battle-sword was, as always, at his side. Two similarly dressed Solonians stood by him. One, a fierce-looking giant of a warrior, was Varan's bodyguard. The other was his son, a younger version of Varan himself. They made a colourful and barbaric trio against the austere metal setting of the transfer area. Standing a little behind them were two black-uniformed Skybase guards, hands close to their blasters.

Varan shivered as he watched the empty cubicles before him. Despite his long familiarity with the Overlords, their magic never failed to impress him. Soon the people now standing in similar booths on

12

the surface of Solos would shimmer and vanish, re-appearing almost instantaneously, here on Skybase. Varan had used the matter-transmitting beam himself, many times, feeling the eerie tugging sensation as the molecules of his body were dispersed, transmitted and reassembled. To him it was magic, and always would be.

(Absorbed in watching the cubicles, Varan failed to notice that something was wrong with his bodyguard. The giant warrior was shivering and sweating. He was making a desperate attempt to conceal his illness and he kept his left hand always hidden beneath his cloak.)

There was a hum of power. More Solonians appeared in the transfer cubicles. Their leader, slim, dark and fierce, stepped from the cubicle. His name was Ky, and he too wore the colourful robes of a War Chief. Ky was much younger than Varan, still in his early twenties. He and Varan bore no love for each other. For one thing their tribes were hereditary enemies. The Solonians had a long tradition of war amongst themselves. But even more important issues were dividing them now. Varan was a supporter of the Overlords, the Earthmen who had ruled Solos for so many generations. Ky was a revolutionary, sworn to overthrow the Overlord regime.

For a moment, Ky and Varan confronted each other. Then Varan said ironically, 'Greetings, Ky!'

Scornfully Ky returned the salutation. 'Greetings, Varan! I knew you would be here—at the heels of your Overlord masters.'

Varan restrained his anger. The Overlords would permit no brawling here on Skybase. 'And why are you here?'

'I was summoned—as you were.'

'You will attend the Conference?'

'Conference!' said Ky bitterly. 'More lies from the Overlords, more promises of freedom that never comes.'

Varan looked hard at him. 'Yet still you came, Ky. Why?'

'To demand that the Overlords cease from murdering our people!'

Ky was referring to the mutations that were sweeping through the people of Solos like some strange disease. First the fever, then the terrifying bodily changes. The Overlords had pronounced that the mutations were caused by a plague, and were ruthless in wiping out all those affected. Varan, as chief native administrator on the planet, had taken a considerable part in this grim work. Yet he was patriotic also, and took no pleasure in the destruction of his own people. His face darkened with anger. 'The Mutants are cursed. They must be rooted out. They are evil, diseased——'

'Who tells us they are evil?' interrupted Ky.

'My eyes tell me ...'

'No, Varan! The Overlords tell you! They tell you to kill—and you kill!'

(A shiver shook the giant figure of the bodyguard and he clamped his cloak-covered left hand closer to his side. Locked in angry confrontation, neither Ky nor Varan noticed him.)

'My people are warriors,' said Varan hotly. 'It is honourable to fight!'

'Where is the honour in hunting down those who are ill and unarmed?'

'They are *diseased*. It is a duty.'

Ky launched into an angry speech. 'If it is a disease, what has caused it? Once we were farmers and hunters. Then the Overlords came, poisoning our planet and calling it progress. We toiled in their mines. We became slaves—and worse than slaves! Like you, Varan!'

Varan's hand went to his sword. 'Liar!' he shouted. Ky's hand was already on his own sword hilt. 'Murderer! You have nothing left to hunt, so you hunt your own kind—Overlord dog!'

With terrifying speed the razor-sharp battle swords flashed from their sheaths. The Skybase guards had their blasters drawn almost as quickly. There was a moment of tense confrontation. Then Stubbs came into the area, summing up the situation at a glance. He sighed wearily. Touchy lot, these Solonians, always at each other's throats. And that young Ky was the worst of the lot. Stubbs waved to the guards to put their blasters away, and stepped casually between the drawn swords. 'Arrived at last, have you, Ky?'

Ky glared at him, then gave a sudden, unexpected smile. There was something almost comic about Stubbs' matter-of-fact tone. He sheathed his sword and gave an ironic bow. 'As you see, Overlord. We come meekly when we are called.'

Stubbs gave him a sceptical look. 'Well don't hang about making speeches. Get through Decontamination. Varan, the Marshal wants to see you—now!'

Ky bowed again and moved through a nearby door, followed by his entourage. Varan's son followed them. Sheathing his sword, Varan moved off in the opposite direction. Automatically, the bodyguard started to follow. Varan waved him back. 'Wait here.' He strode off down the corridor.

Stubbs turned to the two guards. 'You—come with me. You, stay here till you're relieved.' Followed by the chosen guard he disappeared after Varan.

The remaining guard looked warily at the giant Solonian. He was newly posted to Skybase and these wild sword-waving Solonians still made him nervous. He stepped back suddenly as the bodyguard lurched menacingly towards him. But the Solonian staggered past, cannoned blindly into the wall, then slumped to the floor. The guard pulled him roughly to his feet. The bodyguard began struggling wildly, and his left hand came out from beneath his cloak. But it was no longer a hand—it was a huge, reptilian claw!

2

Mutant on the Loose!

The guard jumped back in horror. His fellows had already filled his head with horror stories about the mysterious disease that was sweeping Solos. He'd heard that sufferers sometimes went into a kind of berserk rage, killing everyone in their path. He grabbed for his blaster, but it was too late. A savage blow from the huge reptilian claw clubbed him to the ground.

Tossing the crumpled body of the guard into a cubicle, the Mutant bodyguard lurched off down the corridor.

The Doctor and Jo were still waiting impatiently for the arrival of their non-existent escort. 'Taking their time, aren't they?' grumbled the Doctor.

'Are you sure we're *in* the reception area? Looks more like a broom cupboard to me. And where are we anyway—timewise?'

The Doctor shuddered. 'Please don't use those expressions. According to the TARDIS instruments, we're somewhere in the late thirtieth century Empire period.'

'What Empire?'

'*Your* Empire, Jo. Earth's Empire. Great colonists, the Earthmen. Once they'd sacked the solar system they moved on to pastures new. Solos is one of them. Ever read Gibbon's *Decline and Fall of the Roman Empire*?'

Jo grinned. 'No, but I saw the film.'

'Well, this is like that. Empires rise, empires fall.' Suddenly the Doctor got very cross. 'And if this is their idea of a reception, well it just isn't good enough!' He went over to the door, but it was locked. In no mood to be delayed, the Doctor promptly produced his sonic screwdriver and began dismantling the control panel. 'It's simply a matter of breaking the circuit ...'

There was a sudden shower of sparks and the door slid open. 'You see? Come on, Jo.' Clutching the precious Time Lord despatch box, the Doctor set off down the corridor.

The metallic voice spoke again. 'Attention! Computer confirms door malfunction in Storage Area Three. Security to investigate please.'

Nervously, Jo said, 'You realise that's *us*, Doctor.'

'I know. I don't think I care for being described as a malfunction. Let's try this way, shall we?'

Stubbs and Cotton heard the announcement in the recreation area on the far side of the base. They were immersed in a particularly interesting game of chess. Cotton looked up. 'That's us, Stubbsy. We're on Security stand-by.'

'Go all the way over there for a dodgy door? Seems a bit pointless.'

'Ah, leave it till morning,' grunted Cotton. 'Only just got back after that Mutt-hunt, haven't we? Bet you don't find *him* rushing about tonight.'

Stubbs studied the board. 'Who?'

'His Nibs. Our beloved leader. The Marshal!'

Huge, lavish and highly luxurious, the Marshal's office was his pride and joy. He was leaning forwards over his magnificent desk, whispering urgently to Varan. 'It must be someone we can trust absolutely. Here, he'll need this pass.' He handed Varan a strip of electronically coded plastic.

'And the Overlord weapon?'

'I'll give you that later—at the last possible moment.'

Varan was satisfied. 'It is good.'

The Marshal chuckled. 'Yes, isn't it? By the way, Varan, I shall want to see this man you've chosen— *afterwards.*'

Varan looked puzzled, then nodded. 'You wish to reward him? I will send him to you.'

Varan went silently from the office. The Marshal watched him go, still smiling. What a trusting fool the man was.

The Doctor and Jo moved along the seemingly endless metal corridor that ran round the outer rim of Skybase, making no attempt to conceal their presence. On the contrary.

'Hello, hello!' shouted the Doctor. 'Anyone there?' His voice echoed hollowly. 'This is ridiculous. Are we going to wander round all night without anyone even noticing?'

A locked door across the corridor blocked further progress and Jo looked on resignedly as the Doctor produced his sonic screwdriver yet again. She hoped their unknown hosts weren't going to be too touchy about all this damage.

She heard a deep, hoarse panting somewhere behind her and turned. A huge, fierce-looking native in a tattered robe was moving straight towards them. His right hand clutched a huge curved sword—and the left was a giant claw ...

Jo was so terrified by this sudden apparition that she couldn't even scream. She managed to croak, 'Doctor ... look!'

Still absorbed in his work, the Doctor didn't look up. 'Just a second, Jo ... there!' With another shower of sparks, the door slid free. 'Now then, Jo, what ...'

With a terrifying scream, the giant native raised his sword and charged. 'Look out, Doctor,' yelled Jo.

The Doctor saw the menace and reacted instantly. He slid the door open, shoved Jo through the gap and jumped after her. The sword clanged down against metal in a blow that would have split the Doctor in half.

Once on the other side of the door, the Doctor started trying to slide it shut again. Since he'd just destroyed the locking mechanism, there was no way to *keep* it shut. A giant claw appeared round the edge of the door and began slowly forcing it open ...

'Check,' said Cotton and sat back from the board in satisfaction.

Stubbs was still frowning in concentration when the loudspeaker boomed, '*Second* door malfunction in Storage Area Three. Security investigation please. Computer estimates possible emergency.'

Stubbs stood up. 'Come on. We should have gone the first time.'

Cotton nodded. 'Two malfunctions ... don't like the sound of that, Stubbsy.'

'Come on, then, we're in enough trouble already.'

Strapping on their blasters they set off. Stubbs really wasn't too bothered by the interruption. He'd been losing the chess game anyway.

Palms flat against the metal door, the Doctor heaved with all his strength. It was hard to get a grip on the smooth metal, and their clawed opponent was amazingly strong. Inch by inch the door was sliding open. Jo lent her weight to the struggle, but as her weight was nothing much to speak of, she wasn't much help.

'Get ready to run,' gasped the Doctor. 'Can't ... hold it ... much longer ...'

'What *is* that thing, Doctor?'

'Don't know ... but it isn't ... friendly!'

They heard pounding footsteps and two uniformed men appeared from behind them. Since the Doctor's body blocked the claw from view they assumed the two strangers were trying to escape. Both drew their blasters. Politely, the taller one said, 'Get away from the door, please.'

The Doctor tried to warn them. 'No—we can't ...'

'Away from that door—move!' snapped the second man.

The Doctor moved, pulling Jo with him. The door clanged back and the native charged through screaming, sword raised high above his head.

'Mutt!' yelled Stubbs. Both men fired by reflex, and the double impact smashed the Mutant to the ground.

Stubbs pulled the communicator from his belt. 'Stubbs and Cotton reporting. Investigated malfunction Storage Area Three. Mutant native found and destroyed. Two other non-personnel detained. Message ends.' He turned to Jo and the Doctor. 'Will you accompany us to reception, please?'

The Doctor couldn't help smiling at the formal tone. 'Certainly—though I don't suppose we have any choice.'

'This way, sir.'

The Doctor paused to look at the body of the native. It lay face down and beneath the thin robe, huge reptilian vertebrae were clearly outlined. '*Mutant* native, you said?'

'That's right, sir,' agreed Stubbs politely, and ushered them along the corridor. He spoke quietly to Cotton. 'You tuck these two away, and I'll report to the Marshal. He isn't going to like this—not one little bit!'

The Marshal didn't. 'A *Mutt*—on *my* Skybase,' he screamed. 'How? Why?'

Standing rigidly to attention on the other side of the enormous desk, Stubbs said, 'He came with Varan, sir

—his bodyguard. What about the strangers, sir?'

'Oh, keep them in custody, I've no time for them now ...' He broke off as a tall, grey-haired man came into the room. 'That'll do, Stubbs.' Stubbs saluted and marched thankfully away. The Marshal turned, an expansive smile on his face. 'Ah, there you are, Administrator. Just a little local difficulty, all cleared up now.' The Marshal had no intention of admitting anything was wrong, not in the presence of this distinguished visitor from Earth Council.

The Administrator frowned. 'I hope you're right, Marshal. After all, on the very eve of the Independence Conference ... By the way, I understand Varan arrived here some time before the other Solonian delegates. Why wasn't I informed?'

'I saw no reason to trouble you, sir. Varan had a confidential report to make. He's been keeping an eye on Ky's activities ...'

'Spying for you, you mean?'

The Marshal made a mighty effort to keep his smile in place. 'All a part of security, sir.'

'Good heavens, man, we're not at war with the Solonians. We're giving them independence.'

'Yes, of course, sir. Eventually, eh? Eventually!'

The Administrator had been putting off this moment for some time. But now the Marshal had to be told. 'No, *not* eventually, Marshal. *Now.* Total and absolute independence. We're pulling out.'

'You can't be serious, Administrator.'

'Earth is exhausted, Marshal. Politically, economically, biologically. We cannot afford an Empire any longer.'

The Marshal's mind was racing as he tried to absorb this staggering news. 'We can keep Skybase here,' he suggested. 'Take over the planet completely.'

'Impossible. What about the atmosphere—and the Mutant Solonians?'

The Marshal said eagerly. 'Both are problems that can be solved. I've been working on atmospheric modulations. We've fired several ionisation rockets already, and the atmosphere is definitely changing ...'

'So I hear. Ky has been making constant protests to Earth Council about your efforts—and their results. He says that *you* caused the Mutations.'

Angrily, the Marshal stood up. 'There is no proof that my atmospheric experiments are in any way connected with these outbreaks.'

'Perhaps not. But the Mutations did begin soon after the start of your experiments. Ky's been making political capital out of that fact ever since.'

'Ky's nothing more than a troublemaker. As for the Mutants, they're a menace. They must be wiped out! Exterminated!'

'And that's your alternative to independence—mass murder?'

The Marshal returned to the central issue. Ky, the Mutants, the atmosphere experiments, these were all minor problems. What really mattered was this lunatic decision by Earth Council. 'I tell you, Administrator, we can't give these people independence. They'll starve to death without Earthmen to look after them.'

'Indeed? They managed before we came.' The Administrator's voice hardened. 'In any event, Marshal, they shall have their independence, whether they're ready for it or not. Not for their sakes—for ours!'

Slowly the Marshal sat down. 'But I assumed the Conference would follow the usual line,' he said pleadingly. 'Fob the Solonians off with promises, a few minor concessions. It always worked before.'

'This time I shall concede all Ky's demands. Total independence. You will hand over in the shortest possible time and then return Skybase to Earth.'

The Administrator moved towards the door. The interview was over. The Marshal looked up at him. 'I've put my life into this planet,' he whispered. 'My entire career ... what will happen to *me*—after?'

The Administrator had never really liked the Marshal. In his opinion the fellow was an uncultured oaf, unfit for his high position. 'Ah, well, I'm afraid things are going to be a bit tricky for ex-colonial officials. We're cutting down everywhere, you know. But don't worry, old chap, we'll find you something. The Bureau of Records, perhaps. Something— clerical?' Well pleased with this parting shot, the Administrator left the room.

Alone, the Marshal looked round the enormous office with its massive semi-circular desk. He looked at the mural behind it, showing Earth dominating a cluster of lesser planets. The Marshal loved his office. It was the symbol of his power. He had come to Solos many years ago as a lowly security guard. Step by step he had fought his way to the position of Marshal, with supreme power on Solos.

Now he was to lose it all at one blow. Back on crowded, polluted Earth he would be a nobody, one of a crowd of unemployed officials, without powerful friends or academic qualifications to help him. He would be a *nobody*. As he looked round the lavish office, the Marshal realised that there was nothing, *nothing* he would not do to prevent that happening.

He touched a button on his desk. 'Is Varan there? Send him in immediately.'

Varan hurried into the room, his face filled with fear. 'Lord, in the matter of my bodyguard, I swear I had no idea ...'

The Marshal waved his hand. 'Forget him, the matter is closed. The situation has changed, Varan, I have new instructions for you. Listen carefully.'

Varan listened. As he took in the details of the Marshal's new plan, his face slowly filled with horror.

3

Assassination!

Jo peered out of a porthole and called to the Doctor. 'Look, you can see the planet in daylight now.'

The Doctor rose from his chair and joined her. Far below them hung the mist-shrouded shape of Solos. Jo frowned. 'Not a bit like Earth, is it? It's all grey and foggy.'

'The Earth these people know is even more grey,' said the Doctor sadly. 'Land and sea, all grey. Grey cities linked by grey highways across a grey desert. Ash, clinker, slag—the fruits of technology.'

After a hurried passage through the decontamination area, the Doctor and Jo had been brought to this place and simply left. It wasn't a cell exactly, more likely disused quarters for one of the crewmen. A guard had brought them a simple meal, but he'd refused to answer any of their questions.

Jo turned away from the porthole. 'How much longer will they keep us here?'

'Till they've got time to deal with us, I suppose. I've a feeling we've turned up in the middle of a crisis.'

The door opened and a tall, grey-haired man entered, followed by one of the two guards who'd first found them. It was Stubbs, the shorter, broad-shouldered one. Jo thought he had rather a nice face, for all his obvious toughness.

The tall man was frowning impatiently at them. 'I am the Administrator.'

'Good morning,' said the Doctor politely. 'I'm the Doctor, and this is Jo Grant, my assistant.'

The Administrator didn't care for this interruption. 'I happened to see this guard's report. You will kindly tell me what you're doing here—as briefly as possible, please.'

'Typical bureaucrat,' thought the Doctor to himself. 'Hates anything to disturb his nice routines.' Out loud he said, 'We've come from Earth ...'

'Who sent you?'

The Doctor struggled to remember Earth's political set-up in this period. 'Earth Council.'

'But the Council has no further interest in Solos.'

'Indeed? Well it had when we left. I've a very important message ...'

The Marshal marched in, two security guards behind him. In the rush of preparations for the Conference, not to mention certain secret preparations of his own, he'd forgotten all about the two intruders. Alarmed to hear that the Administrator had decided to question them, the Marshal had come hurrying to find out what was going on. He interrupted the Doctor with brutal abruptness. 'This man is lying. He's got no pass and there have been no shuttle landings on Skybase for some time. Apart from your own, that is, Administrator. I assume you didn't bring them— or did you?'

The Doctor had summed up the Marshal even quicker that he had the Administrator. A brute and a bully, with the temper of a rogue elephant—a very dangerous man. 'Does it matter *how* we arrived?' He produced the despatch-box. 'This is *why* we're here.' He handed the box to the astonished Administrator. To the Doctor's surprise, the box didn't open. 'Ah. Well, it appears it's not for you.'

The Marshal snatched the box and examined it suspiciously. Still nothing happened. 'Nor for you, either,' said the Doctor. He tried to take the box back, but the Marshal snatched it away.

'Is this some kind of joke?' asked the Administrator peevishly. 'What is this object, anyway? For whom is it intended?'

The Doctor said, 'It's a kind of container. And I must confess, gentlemen, I still don't know who it's for ...'

'Open it,' ordered the Marshal.

'I can't. It will only open for the person for whom it is intended.'

'We'll see about that!' Before the Doctor could stop him, the Marshal tossed the box in a corner, drew his blaster and fired. The box glowed brightly in the energy flow. Then the glow faded and the box was as before, quite unharmed.

The Doctor picked it up. It wasn't even charred. 'You see?'

'They were found with the Mutt,' blustered the Marshal. 'They're spies, saboteurs.'

Scornfully the Doctor said, 'If we were, that thing would probably have been a bomb. Thanks to you, we'd all be blown to smithereens by now.'

The Marshal choked with rage. Before he could actually reply a guard entered the room and saluted the Administrator. 'Sir, the Solonian Conference delegates are waiting for you.'

'Thank you. I'll come at once.' The Administrator paused in the doorway. 'Whatever all this is about, it'll just have to wait. I have a Conference to attend.'

When he was gone the Marshal moved closer to the Doctor and Jo, his huge bulk looming menacingly over them. 'Now perhaps you'll let me know what's really going on?'

'We already have,' said Jo. 'The Doctor's telling you the truth.'

The Marshal didn't believe her. 'Who are you really, eh? Secret Agents from Earth Council, sent to check up on me?'

The Doctor waved the box at him. 'If you really want to find out what's in here, take it to this Conference you're having. It could well be intended for someone there.'

The Marshal couldn't make the Doctor out—and what he didn't understand he didn't trust. 'I've got more important things to worry about.' He turned to the guard. 'Stubbs, I'm putting these two in your charge. Don't let them out of your sight.'

Stubbs saluted and the Marshal strode from the room, taking the other guards with him.

So large was the Marshal's office that it could easily double as a small conference hall on occasions such as this.

By the time the Marshal arrived, the room was already crowded. Small groups of Solonian delegates in their colourful robes were scattered about, Ky's supporters in one group, Varan's in another. The chairs for the Administrator and his party were ranged behind the Marshal's desk. A raised dais served as a kind of platform for the official party. Uniformed security men lined the walls and guarded the doors.

The Marshal made his stately way across the room, bowing and smiling at the delegates. When he came to Varan he paused, motioning him to one side. 'Which is your man?'

Varan was tense, almost pale beneath his dark skin. 'Over there, by the door.'

'Does he understand the instructions—the *new* instructions?'

'He understands, Lord.'

'Is he reliable?'

Varan nodded proudly. 'He is Vorn—my son!'

'Your *son*?' For a moment the Marshal frowned. This was an added complication. Then he beamed. 'Excellent, Varan. Give him this.' He slipped a gleaming metallic object from beneath his tunic and passed it to Varan, who concealed it under his robes. Shouldering his way through the crowd, the Marshal took his seat behind the desk. Varan started edging his way across the room towards his son.

An aide called loudly, 'His Excellency the Administrator.' The official party rose, the Solonians ceased their low-voiced chattering and stood in respectful silence. Impressive in his official robes, the Admin-

27

istrator entered through the main doors, flanked by his aides. The Solonian Independence Conference— the *last* Independence Conference—had begun.

Stubbs lounged against the door, keeping no more than a casual eye on the Doctor and Jo. He didn't expect any trouble. The girl was no more than pocket-sized for a start. As for the Doctor chap, he must be getting on a bit, what with that lined face and mop of white hair. The old boy seemed pretty spry for his age, but Stubbs was sure he could handle him. There was a small monitor screen mounted on the wall beside the door and Stubbs switched it on. 'Direct line to the Conference. Might as well see what's going on, eh? Being broadcast all over Solos, this is.'

Stirring martial music came from the screen's loud-speaker and a voice boomed, 'This is an official Over-lord telecast, direct from Skybase.'

The Doctor winced. 'Bit bombastic, isn't it?'

Stubbs shrugged. 'Impresses the natives down on Solos.'

'Does it? I wonder.'

The pompous voice boomed on. 'In a few minutes His Excellency the Administrator will begin his speech to the Delegates of the Solonian All Peoples Union ... Among those present are Paramount Chief Varan, Chief Vorn, his son, Chief Ky ...'

Stubbs winced. 'We know all that, mate.' He reached up and switched off the sound.

The Doctor looked curiously at the crowded scene on the monitor. 'What's your view on all this, Stubbs?'

'Independence? Sooner the better. Then we can all get off home.'

'Ah yes, quite so.' The Doctor looked at Jo and nodded imperceptibly towards Stubbs. Jo realised he wanted her to keep the conversation going.

Brightly she asked, 'Have you got a family back on Earth, Mr Stubbs?'

Stubbs grinned. 'I hope so, miss. It's so long since I've seen them ...'

'I expect you hear from them though?'

'They send the odd video-tape ...'

'No letters?'

'Letters, miss? What kind of letters?'

The Doctor smiled to himself—Jo didn't realise that in this century the hand-written letter was a thing of the past. He strolled across to the monitor, on the pretext of taking a closer look at the screen. Stubbs, absorbed in his conversation with Jo, who was explaining what a letter was, failed to notice that the Doctor was slightly behind him. Suddenly the Doctor said, 'Sorry about this, Stubbs, old chap.' His hand flashed out and Stubbs slid unconscious to the floor.

'Well done, Jo,' said the Doctor.

Jo looked down at Stubbs. 'Pity you had to do that. He seemed rather nice.'

'Did he?' said the Doctor absently. He grabbed the despatch box. 'Come on, Jo, we've got to get to that Conference.'

The Administrator was getting into stride now, droning his way through a rather flowery summary of the long history of Earth–Solos relations. Varan and the pro-Earth Solonians listened respectfully, but Ky and his supporters were becoming steadily more impatient. Ky began making rude and intentionally audible comments. When the Administrator blandly ignored him, Ky began a chant of 'Freedom now! Freedom now! Freedom now!' His supporters took up the cry and soon the Administrator's voice was almost drowned out by the chanting.

By the time the Doctor and Jo reached the Marshal's office, the noise was clearly audible in the corridor outside. They tried to go straight in, but an armed security guard stopped them. 'And where do you think you're going?'

'To the Conference of course,' said the Doctor loftily.

'Got a pass, have you?'

'Well, no, but it's all been cleared with the Administrator. I've an important message ...'

'No one goes in without a pass. Extra security. Now then, let's have a look in that box.'

The Doctor sighed. The chanting from inside the room grew steadily louder.

Inside the room the Administrator was battling on, trying to make himself heard. 'If only you would listen to me. We have no need to quarrel! My friends, Earth Government is prepared to concede ...'

His voice was lost. Ky was on his feet, shouting. 'We have had five hundred years of oppression and slavery. Now you plan to take from us the very air we breathe!'

The Marshal jumped up. 'Guards,' he bellowed. 'Arrest him!' Desperately the Administrator tried to raise his voice above the din. 'Friends, I beg of you ... Listen to me—we have no need to quarrel. Earth Government is prepared to concede your demands. If you would only let me finish ...'

His voice was drowned. Ironically, Ky and his friends were making so much noise that the Administrator was unable to tell them the one thing they had waited so long to hear.

Guards plunged into the milling crowd and tried to arrest Ky. But he was protected by the struggling crowd of his supporters. Fighting broke out, and the Marshal watched the chaotic scene with satisfaction. He caught a glimpse of Vorn, Varan's son, by the door and muttered, 'Now, you fool, *now*!' As if in obedience to this unheard command he saw Vorn slip a hand beneath his robes ...

Over by the door, Vorn felt the cold metal of the dart-gun his father had passed to him. It was stubby and compact, easily concealed in the hand. He drew it out and looked longingly at Ky. To kill Ky, his father's enemy and his own, that had been understandable. But this ... For a moment he hesitated. But his father's new instructions had been clear. And he must obey. Raising the gun Vorn took careful aim at his new target, and fired. There was a soft 'pfft' of compressed air.

On the other side of the room, the Administrator reeled and fell, clutching at the tiny dart embedded in his neck. Vorn slipped the gun beneath his robes and lost himself in the milling crowd.

As soon as the Administrator fell, the Marshal bellowed, 'Ky has killed the Administrator. Arrest him!' More security guards plunged into the fray.

Ky heard the Marshal's bellow and immediately realised his danger. 'Out, all of you,' he yelled. 'This is some Overlord treachery. Back to Solos!' Ky led the dash for the door.

The Doctor was still arguing with the guard, when the doors burst open. A milling crowd of Solonians poured out, Ky at their head. For a moment the Doctor and Ky were jammed together in the crush, the Time Lord despatch-box wedged between them. To the Doctor's astonishment the lid of the box started to open ... He stared at Ky. 'It's for you,' he shouted. 'The message is for *you*!'

Ky thrust him aside. 'Out of my way, Overlord,' he snarled. He ran off down the corridor towards the transfer cubicles.

'Wait,' shouted the Doctor. 'The box is for *you*. I've got to talk to you!' He tried to follow Ky, but the tightly packed mob of guards and Solonians blocked his way.

Jo saw a chance to be useful. 'All right, Doctor,' she called, 'I'll fetch him back for you.' Thanks to her small size she managed to wriggle through the crowd and set off down the corridor after Ky.

The Marshal, a squad of guards behind him, rammed his way out of the doors. 'Get after Ky,' he roared. 'He is an assassin—he must be stopped!' The Doctor found himself caught up in their headlong rush.

Ky was some way ahead by now, Jo close behind him. She followed him down the corridor and around several corners. At last they reached an open area with a row of cubicles; not unlike telephone boxes. Ky paused and Jo caught up with him. '*Please* wait,' she panted, 'I've got to talk to you.'

They heard the sound of pursuing footsteps coming after them. Ky grabbed Jo and dragged her into a cubicle. Jo struggled wildly. 'What do you think you're doing?'

'You are my shield,' explained Ky grimly. 'They will not fire on an Overlord.'

'But I'm not an Overlord. I want to help you!'

The Marshal and his guards, blasters levelled, appeared round the corner—the Doctor was close behind them. 'Stop them,' yelled the Marshal. 'They must be stopped.'

Jo tried to free herself, but in the confined space of the cubicle Ky held her easily. She glimpsed a row of controls with a printed sign above them. 'Have you got your Oxy-mask?' She saw Ky's hand reaching for the controls.

By now half a dozen blasters were trained on the struggling pair in the booth. 'Shoot, you fools,' screamed the Marshal. 'Shoot before they get away.'

The Doctor forced his way to the Marshal's side. 'No, you can't ...'

The Marshal sent him reeling with a brutal shove. 'I said fire. *That is an order!*'

Obediently the guards opened fire. The transfer-booth exploded in flames.

4

Hunted on Solos

As the smoke cleared, the Doctor rushed forward, examining the shattered wreckage. To his immense relief there were no bodies amongst the twisted metal and shattered glass. Ky must have reached the transfer button just in time.

The Marshal reached the same conclusions, and reacted with furious rage. 'Alert Solos ground station. Guards, get after them!' He turned to the Doctor. 'Pity about your young friend, Doctor. I'm afraid she won't get far without a mask!'

As Ky's finger stabbed the controls, Jo felt the tug of the transfer beam, a moment of utter disorientation. She closed her eyes, and when she opened them it seemed as if nothing had happened. She was still in a cubicle, Ky beside her. She looked out and saw that the Marshal and his guards had vanished. Outside was just a bare concrete-walled corridor. She was on Solos!

Ky was shaking her roughly. 'We're going outside. Better put your mask on.'

Jo looked blankly at him.

'You *must* have a mask,' said Ky impatiently. 'All Overlords carry them.'

'That's what I keep telling you. I'm not an Overlord! Anyway, what do I need a mask for?'

'During the hours of daylight the atmosphere of Solos isn't healthy for humans. That's why all Overlords use oxy-masks.'

'What am I going to do?'

'You'll have to stay here. I'm going to make a run for it.'

Jo thought hard. It was clear that Ky was a vital part of the Doctor's plans. She felt it was her job to stay with him, whatever the risks. 'I'm coming with you. The Marshal was shooting at me too, you know. You'll just have to get one of these masks for me.'

Ky stared hard at her. 'I warn you, my life is more important than yours. Not to me, but to Solos, to my people. I may *have* to leave you ...' He broke off, listening tensely. 'Someone's coming ...'

The duty guard on the ground transfer station had just been alerted by the message from Skybase. He came to the row of transfer cubicles and looked around. Everything seemed normal. But a light above the end cubicle was still glowing red—which meant the cubicle had just been used.

Drawing his blaster the guard moved forward. The cubicle seemed empty, but as he got closer, he saw a small, strangely-dressed girl crouching down inside. He reached in and pulled her out. 'All right, where's the other one?'

'Here, Overlord,' said a voice behind him.

The guard spun round and Ky's fist took him beneath the jaw. Ky checked for a mask, but the masks weren't needed indoors and the guard wasn't carrying one. Ky grabbed Jo's hand, and they ran off down the corridor.

Seconds later another guard appeared. He saw the unconscious body of his mate, drew his blaster and set off after the fugitives.

Jo and Ky heard running footsteps behind them. There was a shout of 'You two—come back!' A blaster-bolt sizzled over their heads. They ducked round a corner, ran down a shorter wider corridor, the end of which was blocked by a heavy metal door. Ky began heaving it open. Behind them the running footsteps came nearer. With a final heave Ky opened the door enough for them to get through. He bundled Jo outside and then followed her, slamming the door closed behind them.

Jo found herself outside a low concrete building, dense jungle all around. A thin, white mist floated eerily through the air. Ky was already disappearing into the jungle, and Jo ran after him. The drifting mist seemed to catch at her throat, making her cough.

Communicator to his ear, the Marshal was listening to a report from Solos. Flanked by guards, still clutching his precious despatch-box, the Doctor stood in front of the desk.

The Marshal switched off the set and slammed it down angrily.

'Bad news?' inquired the Doctor politely.

'For you, Doctor, yes! Your friend has escaped onto the surface of Solos—without a mask. We shall find her eventually, of course—or her body.'

The Doctor leaned forward. 'Kindly explain yourself, sir.'

'Didn't you know? During the hours of daylight, no human can travel on the surface of Solos without an oxy-mask. There's a nitrogen isotope in the soil, of a kind unknown on Earth. The ultra-violet rays of the sun produce a poisonous mist.'

'*How* poisonous?' demanded the Doctor.

The Marshal shrugged. 'It depends on so many things ... your friend's constitution, the thickness of the mist, how far and how fast they travel in daylight.' He paused. 'I *could* intensify the search.'

'Then do so at once!'

'Or I could call it off altogether. Let her—escape.'

'Let her die, you mean! You can't possibly do that!'

'I can do as I please, Doctor. Since the assassination of the Administrator, Earth Council has authorised me to place Solos under martial law. *My* law!' The Marshal pointed. 'You tell me that box contains an important message for Ky. I want to see it before he does.'

'That would be quite unethical——'

'Then I shall be forced to recall the men searching for Miss Grant, Doctor,' said the Marshal sadly. 'We're stretched very thin, here on Skybase.'

The Doctor knew he was being blackmailed, but there was nothing he could do about it. 'Very well. I'll try to open it. I'll need laboratory facilities.'

The Marshal beamed. 'And you shall have them, Doctor. If you'll come with me?'

At first Jo found it fairly easy to keep up with Ky. But as they ran along the misty jungle trails, it became harder and harder for her to breathe. She began coughing and choking, gradually falling behind. Finally she slumped to the ground.

Ky hesitated, then turned back. 'Come on. They're after us!'

'Can't,' gasped Jo. 'You go on.'

Ky looked down at her, and something about the tiny figure stirred his compassion. He heaved her up, slung her over one brawny shoulder, and ran on down the trail.

At the head of a squad of guards, Stubbs and Cotton emerged from the jungle transfer station and looked disgustedly round at the misty jungle. Stubbs took a bio-detector from his belt and checked the reading.

'Something over that way ...' He pointed. 'Very faint, though. And there only seems to be one reading.'

Cotton said slowly, 'Maybe the girl's already ...'

'Maybe. Better get after them and find out.'

Stumbling along the trail, Ky paused. His jungle-trained ears could hear faint sounds. Many men were moving along the trail behind him. He moved Jo's head close to his ear. She was hardly breathing at all

36

now. Ky hesitated. Leaving the trail, he plunged deeper into the jungle.

The Marshal showed the Doctor into a surprisingly well-equipped laboratory and waited proudly for his reaction. Although the Doctor was considerably impressed, he was determined not to show it. 'Adequate,' he said disparagingly. 'Not quite what I'd hoped for—but adequate!'

So enormous was the Marshal's vanity that he couldn't bear any part of Skybase to be criticised. 'I'll have you know this is the finest laboratory it was possible to build. Earth itself has no more advanced equipment.'

The Doctor wandered round examining the rows of dials and meters, the complicated control-consoles that lined the equipment-filled room. 'I need a particle-reversal set-up, to turn the box inside out. All this stuff seems geared to atmosphere modulation. What are you doing here, weather control?'

'Something like that,' replied the Marshal evasively. 'Now then, Doctor . . .'

The Doctor spotted a reading climbing dangerously high. 'Well, *this* is about to overload for a start!' His hands flicked over controls and the reading dropped to below the safety margin.

Immediately, a tubby moon-faced man in the eternal white coat of the scientist rushed angrily into the laboratory. Untidy grey hair stuck up wildly, and his accent was so thick as to be almost incomprehensible.

'Who has been tampering with the circuits?' demanded the newcomer angrily.

'I'm afraid it was me,' admitted the Doctor. 'You were about to overload.'

The newcomer turned angrily on the Marshal. 'My experiments have reached a crucial stage, I work alone and against time ... and you lay on some stupid guided tour!'

'That's enough out of you, Jaeger,' rumbled the Marshal.

'You give full priority to atmospheric regeneration, then expect me to ...'

'Jaeger!' The warning threat in the Marshal's voice was unmistakable, and this time Jaeger subsided. The Marshal took him by the arm. 'I want you to switch priorities for the moment to another little problem.' He tapped the Doctor's box. 'The Doctor here will explain.'

The Marshal's communicator set bleeped and he took it from his belt. 'Yes?'

'Varan's son is waiting in your office, Marshal.'

'Good. I'm on my way. Give the Doctor every help, Professor Jaeger. Doctor, you keep me informed about your progress—and I'll keep you informed about Miss Grant.'

The line of guards pounded along the trail, Stubbs and Cotton at their head. As they passed a particularly dense clump of bushes Ky sprang silently forward, crooked an arm round the last guard's neck and pulled him down. The rest of the squad ran on, not realising they were now one short. There was a brief thrashing in the bushes, then silence.

'Why have I been brought here a prisoner?' demanded Vorn angrily.

'A prisoner?' cried the Marshal in mock surprise. 'Of course not, my dear Vorn. See, I send away my guards.' He dismissed them with a wave of his hand.

Once they were alone Vorn said in a low voice. 'It was on *your* orders I killed the Administrator. *You* told my father he was an enemy of our people.'

'You have done well, Vorn, and you shall be rewarded.' The Marshal held out his hand and Vorn handed over the little dart-gun. The Marshal smiled. 'Now for your reward.'

Varan strode angrily towards the Marshal's office, furious at the news of his son's arrest. Guards barred his way at the door.

The dart-gun seemed tiny in the Marshal's enormous hand. 'Useful little device,' he chuckled. 'And most efficient.' The smile disappeared from his face, he raised the gun and Vorn backed away, his eyes widening . . .

'Let me pass,' demanded Varan. 'My son has been arrested—I must see him.' He charged like an angry elephant, smashing the guards aside.

Just inside the doors, Varan paused in unbelieving horror. The Marshal stood by his desk, dart-gun in hand, Vorn's body at his feet.

Slowly Varan walked forward. The Marshal looked up. 'First he assassinated the Administrator,' he said sadly. 'Then he tried to kill me. He must have been in league with Ky all along.'

'You lie, Overlord,' said Varan hoarsely.

The Marshal smiled. 'Earth Council will believe me.' He raised the dart-gun.

Varan sprang to one side, scooped up a heavy chair and flung it at the Marshal's head. It took him on the shoulder, knocking him off his feet. Outside the office guards were just picking themselves up when Varan hurtled into them, sending them flying again. He disappeared down the corridor.

The Marshal struggled to his feet, rubbing his bruised shoulder, and reached for his communicator. 'Attention Skybase. This is the Marshal. The Solonian

Chief Varan has gone Mutant. He is at large on Sky-base armed and dangerous. Do not attempt to capture. Shoot on sight.'

He flicked the communicator on to another circuit. 'Marshal calling Solos. Stubbs, Cotton, come in.'

Stubbs and Cotton stood by the trail, looking down at the unconscious body of one of their guards. Realising Ky was no longer ahead of them, and that one of their men was missing, they had sent out patrols to search and then turned back. As they returned along the trail, Cotton had noticed a boot protruding from the bushes ...

Stubbs was talking into his communicator. 'Come back, sir? But we're almost on them. I've sent the lads out on patrol.'

There was a pause, then the Marshal's voice crackled from the set. 'All right, *one* of you up here immediately to hunt down Varan, the other stay and organise the search for Ky. Marshal out!'

The set went dead. Stubbs and Cotton looked at each other.

'You stay here, all right?' said Stubbs.

Cotton nodded sourly. 'Thanks a lot. Hey, Stubbsy, someone's pinched the poor bloke's oxy-mask.'

'Yeah, I noticed. I'll send the medics down to pick him up. See you.'

Stubbs disappeared down the trail. Left alone, except for the unconscious guard, Cotton looked uneasily round the misty jungle. Ky could be anywhere out there, waiting to spring ...

He reached for his communicator and started checking the patrols. Soon reports were coming in ... Ky and the girl had been spotted ... moving towards the mines ...

5

The Experiment

The Doctor and Professor Jaeger were hard at work. It wasn't a happy collaboration. Jaeger resented having to give time to the Doctor's concerns. His resentment was worsened by the high-handed way in which the Doctor had appropriated several of his valuable pieces of equipment, cannibalising them and linking them together in an incredibly complicated electronic lash-up, its purpose, if it had one, defeating Jaeger completely. Reduced to the status of a lab assistant, he sulkily linked circuits and tested connections under the Doctor's direction.

The Doctor seemed to be in a sunny mood, chatting idly as he worked. 'Can't think why you people ever came to Solos in the first place.'

Jaeger grunted. 'Thaesium, Doctor. Solos is one of the richest fuel sources in the galaxy. Or rather it used to be. The deposits are exhausted now.'

'So you plan to colonise the planet in earnest—*if* you can change the atmosphere?'

Jaeger frowned suspiciously. 'That's my concern, Doctor, not yours.'

'The Solonians, too. It's their planet.'

'It *was* their planet. Doctor—you did say Doctor, didn't you?'

The Doctor checked the circuit Jaeger was working on, found the connection was faulty, moved Jaeger aside and finished the job himself. 'There, that's better,' he said reprovingly. 'We'll need that to hold the Proton beam *steady*—Professor.'

Jaeger said sourly, 'This whole thing's a waste of time. No one's ever achieved particle reversal—it's still only theory ...'

The Doctor made a few final adjustments and

stepped back, studying his creation with satisfaction. The final effect was rather like a giant microscope. 'On the contrary, old chap, I find it a very useful research technique.' He took the box and put it on a small raised platform in the centre of the apparatus.

Jaeger looked scornfully at the ramshackle assemblage of equipment. 'And what do you hope to achieve by all this?'

'I expect the particles to reverse,' explained the Doctor patiently. 'What is outside will be on the inside, and what is inside will be on the outside—where we can see it!'

'Rubbish!'

The Doctor grinned. 'You'd better come over here and see for yourself.' He moved to the on/off switch, which he had prudently rigged up at some distance from the apparatus. The Doctor threw the switch and, to Jaeger's astonishment, he saw the box glow, shimmer, and dissolve into a pile of ancient-looking scrolls and dusty parchments. There was a bang, a flash, and a puff of smoke. One of the circuits blew and the box was a box again.

The Doctor sighed and moved over to the apparatus. Gingerly he touched the blackened circuit. 'Ah well, always a snag or two at first!'

'But it worked,' said Jaeger incredulously.

'Well of course it worked. Did you see what was inside?'

'I got a glimpse of some kind of ancient documents ... But the process, Doctor. It actually worked.'

The Doctor nodded. 'All over in a flash, you might say!'

They were interrupted by the Marshal. He marched into the laboratory, Stubbs at his heels, and glared round suspiciously. 'Have you seen any sign of Varan?'

The Doctor looked blankly at him. 'Have I seen who?'

42

'Jaeger—have you seen him? Varan—the Mutt. We've had reports he was seen heading this way.'

The Doctor's scientific interest was aroused. 'A Mutant? Here on Skybase? I'd very much like to see him.'

Impatiently the Marshal barked, 'Well, Jaeger?'

Jaeger was still studying the Doctor's apparatus, trying to fathom its secret. 'No, I haven't seen Varan, I've got more important things to worry about.'

'Like the Doctor's mysterious box? How are you getting on?'

Before Jaeger could answer, Stubbs' communicator bleeped. He listened, then turned to the Marshal. 'They think they've spotted Varan in the Seed Propagation Area, sir.'

'All right, Stubbs, you know what to do.'

Stubbs was about to go when the Doctor said, 'Just a moment. I'd very much like to join on this ... hunt.'

'Out of the question,' barked the Marshal.

Jaeger intervened. 'I'm sure the Doctor would find it most interesting, Marshal. And I'd like a word with you.'

The Marshal looked hard at him. Clearly Jaeger wanted the Doctor out of the way. 'Very well, you can go, Doctor. Keep an eye on him, Stubbs.'

Stubbs rubbed his neck meaningfully. 'Don't worry, sir, this time I will.'

When the Doctor and Stubbs had gone, the Marshal swung round on Jaeger. 'Well?'

Jaeger moved closer and whispered excitedly. 'With the Doctor's help I could have the atmosphere regeneration project operational within a week.' Briefly he described the Doctor's experiment. 'He *built* a particle reversal set-up from the odds and ends—and it *worked*. With that kind of scientific knowledge, and with particle reversal, we can short-cut the entire process.'

'Then we must make sure he continues to co-operate.' The Marshal smiled. 'His assistant is the key—we must find that young lady, Jaeger—and quickly.'

Jo awoke to find herself in semi-darkness. Something smooth and plastic was being pressed gently to her lips. Eagerly she breathed in the life-giving oxygen.

Ky took away the oxy-mask. 'Steady, not too much at first.'

'Where are we?' whispered Jo. 'Is it a cave?'

'A man-made cave. It's an abandoned mine, that runs beneath one of our mountains.'

Jo looked round. In the dim greenish light that filtered from the entrance to the shaft, she could see rough rock walls, and pit-props supporting the roof. They were just inside the entrance of a long, square-cut tunnel that ran slantingly down into darkness.

Ky looked thoughtfully at her. 'You are from Earth—yet you say you are not an Overlord ... why did you come here?'

'We came to help you. The Doctor says—'

'The Doctor—he is the Overlord with the box?'

'For heaven's sake—we're *not* Overlords!' said Jo exasperatedly.

'I'm sorry. My people know Earthmen only as Overlords. It is difficult to think otherwise. Why did this —Doctor try to give me the box?'

'There's something inside that's intended for you. That's why I followed you, to tell you.'

'What is it? Weapons?'

'I don't know. You'll have to ask the Doctor.'

Ky smiled ruefully. 'How?'

Jo looked around. How indeed, she thought. Hopefully she said, 'The Doctor will find us.'

Ky nodded, but he didn't look convinced. 'Perhaps. We must stay in hiding for a while. If the Doctor comes, my people will tell us.'

Ky began questioning Jo about Earth, but since her account of twentieth century Earth didn't fit in with all he'd heard about Earth in the thirtieth cen-

44

tury, Jo hurriedly changed the subject. She asked about the Mutants.

Ky explained that in recent years a strange disease had been spreading through the Solonian people. The victims suffered horrifying bodily changes —mutations. Their hands turned to claws, their spines grew curved and knobbly, and finally they changed into a creature that looked like a giant insect. Ky and his supporters believed that pollution from the technology Earthmen had brought to Solos was responsible—that, and some mysterious experiments in atmosphere-changing being carried out by the Marshal.

Jo shuddered. 'What happens to people—after they've changed to Mutants?'

'The Marshal has declared the Mutations are a disease—a plague. He and his men hunt down the Mutants and kill them. Mutts, they call them ... *Mutts!* Those who escape hide in darkness—in places like this.'

From the darkness further down the tunnel there came a scuttling.

The Doctor followed Stubbs down the endless metal corridors of Skybase. The place was enormous, he realised, a city in the sky. Since Earth had been running down its forces for some time now, much of Skybase was unused. It wouldn't be easy to find just one native in this maze of corridors and empty rooms.

'Sure you want to come?' asked Stubbs. 'Could be dangerous.' He paused outside a heavy metal door.

The Doctor nodded. 'After you, Mr Stubbs.'

Stubbs touched a control and the door slid back. They entered a huge echoing chamber, very hot, dimly lit with a greenish glow. All around were rows upon rows of tall green plants. The dripping of water echoed hollowly in the semi-darkness. It was like an indoor jungle—a natural hiding place for Varan.

45

The Doctor looked round. 'What's this place for—seed propagation, did you say?'

Stubbs nodded. 'They were trying to adapt Earth crops for Solos. Never worked. All abandoned now, of course.' He drew his blaster and they advanced into the shadowy darkness between the long rows of plants. Stubbs began calling, 'Varan? Come on out, old son. May as well get it over quickly. We know you're here ...'

There was no reply. They moved deeper into the plant-rows.

'What do you mean, get it over?' whispered the Doctor. 'You're not going to shoot him in cold blood?'

'Only way, Doctor. You haven't seen what they turn into.'

The Doctor looked hard at Stubbs, but said nothing.

Stubbs moved on. 'Come on, Varan. Make it easy on yourself. Come on, Varan, answer me!'

Stubbs got his answer sooner than he expected. Varan hurtled over a row of plants, sword in hand, landed on top of him, and knocked the blaster from his hand. Stubbs went down grappling desperately with Varan's sword-arm. The Doctor jumped over their struggling bodies and grabbed for the fallen blaster.

Varan was gaining the upper hand. He pinioned Stubbs to the ground, and wrenched his sword-arm free. 'Varan is no Mutt, Overlord,' he snarled. 'I am a warrior! Now die!'

Varan raised the sword for a killing blow and the Doctor shouted, 'No wait! Let him go!' Berserk with fury, Varan paused and glared wildly at the Doctor. He raised his sword again. The Doctor fired, blasting the sword from Varan's hand. The shock seemed to bring Varan to his senses. Releasing Stubbs, he climbed slowly to his feet.

Stubbs got up too. 'I'll take that blaster, Doctor.' The Doctor hesitated. 'Hand it over,' said Stubbs grimly. The Doctor seemed to fumble with the blaster and almost dropped it. Stubbs snatched it from his hand, and levelled it at Varan.

'Don't be a fool, Stubbs,' shouted the Doctor. '*Look* at him. Do you see any signs of mutation?'

Stubbs looked. Both Varan's hands were normal, and there were no tell-tale Mutant ridges along the spine. Slowly Stubbs said, 'But the Marshal said he'd gone Mutant ...'

'The Marshal murdered my son,' bellowed Varan. He sprang forward, snatched the blaster and levelled it at Stubbs' head. 'Now you shall die, as my son died,' he shouted—and pulled the trigger.

Nothing happened. The Doctor stepped quickly forward and took the blaster from Varan's unresisting hand. 'I put it on safety. There's been too much killing already. Now I think you'd better tell us your story, Varan. We're your only hope.'

Varan's berserk fury collapsed as swiftly as it had come, as he stumblingly told the story of the Marshal's schemes. In the dank silence of the huge plant room, the Doctor and Stubbs listened to the horrifying tale of treachery and murder. 'At first the plan was to kill Ky. Then it was changed. The Marshal told us that the Earth Lord was our real enemy. We obeyed and killed him. Then the Marshal killed my son ...' Varan's voice broke in anguish.

'After that he would have executed you,' said the Doctor. 'Then no one would have known the real truth.'

'Why?' burst out Stubbs. 'I can understand knocking off Ky. But why the Administrator?'

'I imagine the Administrator planned to give the Solonians the independence they wanted. The days of Earth's Empire are drawing to a close. And with Solos independent ...'

'His Nibs would be out of a job,' concluded Stubbs.

'He would indeed. Now, with the Administrator

47

murdered by "terrorists", independence is bound to be delayed. The Marshal will use that time to seize control of the planet. Eventually he'll declare its independence from Earth—under *his* rule!'

Stubbs was very quiet for a moment, taking it all in. Almost to himself he said, 'So what do I do now?'

'That depends which side you're on, Stubbs.'

Stubbs drew a deep breath. 'I reckon I've had just about enough of the Marshal. I'm with you, Doctor.'

'Then the first thing you must do is report back to the Marshal—to tell him Varan has been destroyed.'

Cotton stood rigidly to attention before the Marshal's desk, concluding his report. The Marshal was far from pleased. 'I am surrounded by incompetents,' he roared.

'At least it seems the girl's still alive, sir,' said Cotton desperately. 'But it'll take a lot of men to search those mine-workings.'

'Exactly. And meanwhile Ky's got her. Not us! Send more patrols after them. I want that girl found. And Cotton ...'

'Sir?'

'As far as the Doctor is concerned, she *has* been found. Got it? *You* found her, Cotton. She was in a bad way, and she's in hospital, on Solos. Got it?'

'Yes sir,' said Cotton, not getting it at all.

Stubbs came in, the Doctor close behind him. 'Varan located and dealt with, sir,' he said.

The Doctor decided to add a bit of conviction to the story. He glared at Stubbs in pretended anger. ' "Dealt with" indeed. Murdered more like it!'

'An unfortunate necessity,' said the Marshal smoothly. 'These matters are more of a menace than you realise, Doctor—as Miss Grant will no doubt tell you, when she recovers.'

'You've found her? Is she hurt? When can I see her?'

The Marshal said meaningfully. 'Cotton!'

Cotton stared and said woodenly, 'The young lady's on Solos, sir. Receiving oxygen treatment. It'll be a day or two before she can be moved.'

'Possibly longer,' said the Marshal hurriedly. 'Ky abandoned her, left her to die. She was pretty far gone when Cotton found her. Meanwhile, Doctor, Professor Jaeger needs your assistance on a project of some urgency. It will pass the time——'

'Until you decide to let me see Miss Grant?'

'Precisely, Doctor. Now then, shall we return to the laboratory?' The Marshal paused by the door. 'You know, Doctor, I've got the strangest feeling. The quicker your experiments succeed—the quicker Miss Grant will recover! So work hard, won't you, Doctor? The young lady's life may be at stake.'

6

Escape

Jaeger stood poised before a map of Solos, a pointer in his hand. '... And so you see, Doctor, I plan to bombard the atmosphere of Solos with ionisation rockets. This will create an atmospheric barrier against the ultra-violet rays which produce the poison mists.'

'What you are proposing, Professor,' said the Doctor indignantly, 'is an all-out rocket attack upon an undefended planet.'

Jaeger gave him a pitying look. 'These aren't military rockets, Doctor. They'll explode in the atmosphere ...'

'Try telling the Solonians that,' said the Doctor grimly.

'I don't understand your concern, Doctor. The planet as it stands is no longer of any use—the mineral deposits are exhausted. We must make the atmosphere breathable for humans ...'

'Even if you risk wiping out the Solonians in the process? Suppose your new atmosphere doesn't suit them?'

'There may be certain side-effects ...'

'You should write a paper on that, Professor—genocide as a side effect.'

'Perhaps you have an alternative suggestion?'

'Perhaps.'

'Using particle reversal, no doubt?' sneered Jaeger.

'Particle reversal is one way,' agreed the Doctor calmly. 'Not as quick or as violent as your rockets, but just as effective in the long run ... If we could produce a chain-reaction of atmospheric modulation ...' The Doctor talked on for some while, blinding Jaeger with a flood of figures and formulae. In fact he was deliberately talking scientific nonsense. He had no intention of helping with the Marshal's experiments. But Jaeger, who wasn't nearly as clever as he liked to think he was, didn't realise that. He was a vain and unprincipled man, desperate for scientific recognition, but without the talent to attain it on his own. A nasty scandal over research results, stolen from a junior colleague, had led to Jaeger's fleeing Earth and entering the Marshal's service. He was filled with excitement at the thought of being known as the man who changed the atmosphere on Solos. The Doctor's part could always be played down in the reports ... perhaps forgotten altogether.

When the Doctor finished, Jaeger said impatiently, 'Yes, yes, Doctor, but can it actually be done?'

'We shall have to set up another experiment,' began the Doctor.

Cotton came into the laboratory, an air of suppressed excitement about him. He stopped short, stared at Jaeger and said, 'Er ... yes. The Marshal wants to see you right away, Professor.'

'Can't it wait?'

'You know the Marshal.'

Jaeger did. He hurried out of the laboratory.

Cotton moved over to the Doctor. 'Sir, I've just had a long chat with Stubbs. He's kind of a mate of mine.'

'Oh yes,' said the Doctor cautiously.

'He told me about Varan.'

'Do you feel the same way about the Marshal as he does?'

Cotton nodded. 'Me and Stubbs always stick together.'

'Then will you take me to see Jo Grant?'

'That's just it, sir, I can't. We didn't find her. As far as I know, she's still with Ky. We reckon they must have gone underground, to the old Thaesium mines.'

The Doctor rubbed his chin. 'So now I've got to find both of them. How am I going to do that, eh, Cotton?'

'No idea, sir. The guards won't let you near the transfer cubicles—and there's no other way down to Solos.'

The Doctor had a sudden inspiration. 'What would happen if I blew the main power supply for all Skybase?'

'Sheer chaos to start with. Then they'd switch to emergency supply, till things were sorted out.'

'But if the emergency supply to the transfer section was *already* switched on ...'

'You could slip down to Solos in the confusion!'

'Exactly, my dear Cotton. Now, can you switch the emergency power on for me?'

'I can try, sir.'

Cotton broke off as Jaeger stormed back into the laboratory. 'Cotton, did you say the Marshal wanted to see me?'

'That's right, sir.'

'Then one of you is mad, Cotton. He drove me away with curses, told me to get back to work!'

'Must have changed his mind, sir.'

'Perhaps you'd better do as he says,' added the Doctor. 'I've been thinking about our particle reversal experiment, Professor Jaeger ... We'll need a colossal amount of power.' The Doctor looked innocently at Cotton. 'Perhaps you could ask the Marshal to arrange for the laboratory to be linked through to the main power supply?'

Some hours later the Doctor was presiding over an increasingly complicated experimental set-up that seemed to include practically every piece of equipment in the laboratory. Jaeger looked on, worried, but not daring to interfere.

Cotton made his way to the transfer section cubicles and waved an impressive clipboard at the duty guard.

'Main power's being diverted for a lab experiment. You're to switch over to emergency circuits now.' Obediently the guard operated the controls. The lit-up cubicles went dark for a moment, and then came to life again.

Stubbs slipped into the gloomy shadows of the seed propagation section. 'Varan? Varan, are you there?'

Varan appeared silently from amongst the plants, his face sullen and suspicious, his drawn sword in his hand.

Stubbs kept very still, keeping his hand well away from his blaster. 'We're going to try to get you off Skybase, Varan. You and the Doctor. When the time comes, make for the transfer cubicles.'

'How will I know when it is time?'

'There'll be a power failure. The lights will go out and then come on again.'

'When will this happen?'

'That's it—we just don't know. Soon, I hope.'

'Is this some Overlord trick?'

Stubbs sighed. 'You'll have to trust us, Varan.' He moved quietly away.

Varan stared after him, his face filled with suspicion. Since the Marshal's treachery and the death of his son, Varan was not inclined to trust any Overlord. But he was sure of one thing. If there was a chance of escape, he would take it—and it would be the worse for anyone who got in his way.

Jaeger was studying the Doctor's amazing assemblage of equipment with increasing alarm. 'Surely a set-up like this will overload the power supply?'

'Not a bit of it, old chap, the modulator's utterly reliable.' The Doctor pointed to a complicated-looking junction point where several circuits met.

'I'd be obliged if you'd keep a close eye on this point here for me.'

Obediently Jaeger leaned over the knotty tangle of wires.

'Splendid,' said the Doctor happily. 'Now if you're ready?'

Jaeger nodded, and the Doctor reached for the main power switch. 'Right!'

The Doctor threw the switch and power hummed through the apparatus. As the power built up the whole ricketty structure began to throb and shake alarmingly. Wisps of smoke drifted up from the overheated circuits.

Jaeger looked up in alarm. 'Doctor, shouldn't we close it down?'

'It's all right,' shouted the Doctor cheerily. 'Just you keep watching that junction-point.'

Jaeger watched—and at that moment the junction-point exploded. The shock threw him clear across the room, and immediately all the lights went out.

The Doctor ran for the door and out into the darkened corridor. All over Skybase he could hear the sound of alarms, voices shouting in confusion. After a moment the officious voice of the computer came over the tannoy. 'Skybase One, we have a power failure. Please remain exactly where you are. Emergency lighting circuits are already coming into service.'

The Doctor had no intention of remaining where he was. He raced down the corridor towards the transfer cubicles.

Following Stubbs' instructions, Varan moved cautiously out into the corridor. It was sheer bad luck that he ran straight into a patrolling guard, who was tense and panicky in the sudden darkness. When the guard saw Varan moving towards him, he fired instinctively. The energy-bolt flashed past Varan's head, and he turned and ran down the corridor, ducking and weaving as he ran through the darkness. As the blaster bolts flashed all around him, Varan's worst suspicions were confirmed. The escape plan of the Overlord Stubbs had been an ambush after all. They were trying to kill him!

The Doctor reached the transfer cubicles at last, slipping past several guards who were milling about confusedly in the darkness. As he stepped into the nearest cubicle a powerful figure seized him from behind. 'Now you shall pay for your treachery,' hissed Varan. 'Die, Overlord! Die!'

The Doctor struggled forward into the cubicle, dragging Varan with him by main force. Inside the cramped cubicle Varan couldn't draw his sword. Instead he clamped both hands round the Doctor's throat and concentrated on throttling him. Unable to break the iron grip, the Doctor groped for the transfer control.

He found it at last, and stabbed desperately for the transfer button. There was a hum of power and suddenly the booth was empty. In the cubicle on Solos, two wildly struggling figures suddenly materialised. They erupted from the booth still fighting. Varan went for his sword and the Doctor closed with him. To his surprise Varan found that this tall thin Overlord had a grip as powerful as his own. His arm was seized, twisted and pinioned behind him in a way that held him completely immobile. 'Now listen, Varan,' panted the Doctor. 'I am *not* an Overlord and I've come to Solos to help your people. I must find Ky.'

Varan winced with pain as he tried to break free and failed. 'Ky is my enemy,' he muttered. 'I shall kill him and you—Overlord.'

He thrashed about wildly, then froze again as the Doctor tightened his hold. 'Varan—either you take me to the disused mines, or we both stay here, like this, till guards from Skybase come and recapture us. Well? Will you give me your word—as a warrior and a chief?'

With some difficulty Varan managed a nod.

'That's the idea,' said the Doctor cheerfully, and released his captive. Varan straightened up, rubbing his arm, and led the way towards the exit.

As they moved along the corridor there was a sudden crash of thunder which seemed to shake the little building.

'Firestorms,' muttered Varan fearfully. 'The gods are angry.'

The Doctor smiled. 'Just a simple atmospheric disturbance, Varan old chap. May come in useful— it'll make searching for us more difficult. Let's get moving, before the duty guard wakes up.'

The thunder was louder as they opened the main door, and there was lightning streaking through the night sky. Varan paused again. 'You have no oxymask. Once the sun rises, you will find it hard to breathe. No Earthman can breath the air of Solos.'

'And who said I was an Earthman?' Smiling at Varan's astonished face the Doctor added, 'Don't worry about me, old chap. Just lead the way to those mines.'

Jo and Ky were watching the lightning from the mouth of their disused mine-shaft.

Ky had built a little fire, and they sat huddled over it watching the lightning flash across the night sky, listening to the thunder which seemed to shake the ground beneath them. 'These firestorms rage all night,' said Ky. 'Each one seems longer and more violent than the last. The people are terrified.'

Jo looked puzzled. 'Aren't they used to thunderstorms by now?'

Ky shook his head. 'Before the Marshal began his experiments, there *were* no firestorms. He plans to make our air breathable for humans ... not for Solonians. It will mean the end of my people ...'

A scream from Jo interrupted him. A huge misshapen figure had appeared from the darkness outside. It moved in a crouch, its back arched and scaly, with huge, knobbly vertebrae. It had a goggle-eyed insect-like head, and two enormous claws. Jo realised she was seeing her first full Mutant.

Claws flexing, the Mutant shambled towards them.

7

The Attack

Ky rose and walked calmly towards the Mutant. 'It's all right. They're quite harmless ...' Suddenly the giant insect-like shape made a rush for him, claws snapping. Ky jumped back, snatched a burning branch from the fire and waved it at the Mutant. Snarling, it retreated into the darkness. Ky came back to the fire. He was badly shaken. 'I don't understand. Usually they run away.'

Suddenly there was another attack—two Mutants rushed forward this time. Again Ky beat them off. With an angry chittering, they fell back into the darkness.

'I thought you said they were harmless,' said Jo.

Ky shook his head, puzzled. 'I've never seen them like this. Perhaps it's the firestorm. Anyway, they seem to be massing out there. We might be safer further back. There's a big natural chamber deeper inside.'

Jo didn't really see why they should be, but she grabbed a burning branch of her own from the fire and followed Ky into the darkness of the inner shaft.

Soon they were in the chamber Ky had told her of, a natural cave that had been incorporated into the mine. But as soon as they retreated, more Mutants flooded forward from the darkness outside. They could hear their claws scrabbling and clattering on the rocks, and the flickering light from the torches illuminated a seething mass of the huge insectoid shapes. Ky looked round, worried, and spotted a tiny fissure in the rocks. 'I think you'd better hide in there,' he said. 'The Mutants won't really harm me, but you're a stranger. Wait here, till I've driven them off!'

The fissure was no more than a tiny crack in the rock wall. There was just room for Jo to squeeze inside.

Once she was safely installed, Ky took her torch. Then, yelling wildly, a blazing torch in each hand, he charged the advancing army of Mutants. They broke before his rush, turned and fled in panic from the cave. Ky chased them up the mine shaft and out into the darkness. He went back to the fire to get fresh torches. His woodpile was already low, but there was no chance of gathering more. Outside the cave the angry chittering sound was growing steadily louder. The Mutants were gathering in force. Soon they would nerve themselves for another rush.

In the dim glow of the emergency-lighting, the Marshal looked at Jaeger and shook his head in disgust. 'A booby-trap. Professor Jaeger, one of the Empire's finest scientific minds, foiled by a simple booby-trap.'

The wild-haired figure slumped on the stool beside him looked up despairingly. Lab coat tattered, hair and eyebrows singed, face blackened, Professor Jaeger was feeling distinctly persecuted. 'He *said* it was a particle reversal experiment,' he muttered defensively.

The Marshal snorted. 'A booby-trap—and you were the booby, Jaeger. Well, forget about the Doctor —I'll take care of him. You concentrate on getting those ionisation rockets ready.'

Perhaps Jaeger's remnants of conscience had been stirred by the Doctor's earlier reproaches. He made a feeble effort to protest. 'I'm just not ready, Marshal. The whole process is still in the experimental stage. It could get out of hand, set off a chain reaction that would make the air on Solos unbreathable for Earthmen or Solonians.'

The Marshal crashed a big fist down on the bench, rattling the equipment. 'Just you get this into your maundering egg-head, Jaeger. I want the atmosphere of this planet modified, and I want it done now! Understand?'

Jaeger nodded, too terrified to protest further. Satisfied, the Marshal reached for his communicator. 'Get me Stubbs and Cotton. I'll be in my office.'

Marching smartly along the corridor, Stubbs and Cotton did their best to look confident. Stubbs said quietly, 'This is it, then!'

Cotton nodded. 'Reckon he's on to us?'

'Soon find out, won't we?'

Marching smartly in step, the picture of military efficiency, they strode through the door of the Marshal's office and came to a halt before his desk.

For a moment the massive figure behind the desk ignored them. Then the great head was raised. 'Ah, Stubbs, Cotton. My trusty right-hand men,' purred the Marshal. There was a smile on the heavily-jowled face, but the eyes were cold and hard. 'So, not content with failing to capture Ky, or Miss Grant, you have now managed to allow the Doctor to escape as well.'

'*We* tried to stop him,' said Stubbs, virtuously.

'That's right, sir,' confirmed Cotton. 'Professor Jaeger let him get away.'

'Silence!' roared the Marshal.

Trying to look injured and innocent, Stubbs and Cotton fell silent.

'We are all going to pay a little visit to Solos,' growled the Marshal. 'While we are there we shall kill three birds with one stone. Ky, the Mutts—and the Doctor.'

When Varan and the Doctor reached the mine-shaft the fire was burning very low, and there was nobody in sight. 'Somebody's been here,' said the Doctor thoughtfully. 'I wonder why they left.'

'Look,' said Varan suddenly, and pointed.

The Doctor turned. In the dim glow of the dying

60

fire he caught sight of a huge insect-shape scuttling
away into the shadows.

'You saw?' said Varan. 'The creatures are evil, diseased.'

The Doctor tapped the Time Lord's despatch-box.
'Perhaps the answer to this outbreak of Mutations is
in here. We must find Ky.'

'Find him alone, Doctor. Varan goes no further.'

The Doctor held up his hand. 'Listen!'

From deeper in the mine came the sounds of a confused struggle. They heard shouts and yells, and a
high-pitched angry chittering sound. 'Something's
going on down there. Maybe Jo's in trouble.' The
Doctor snatched a long branch from a wood-pile by
the fire and kindled the end in the blaze. 'Well, come
on, Varan. Or is the mighty warrior afraid of the
dark?'

'Varan fears nothing!'

'I'm delighted to hear it. Let's go, shall we?'

Torch held high, the Doctor set off down the
tunnel. Varan hesitated for a moment, then made
himself a torch and hurried after the Doctor.

Deeper in the mines, Ky was under siege. The
Mutants had attacked in ever-increasing numbers,
driving him down the mine-shaft and back to the inner
cave. Now they surrounded him, making their angry
high-pitched chittering sound. Ky swung his torches
in great circles, driving them back. But they always
returned, pressing a little closer each time. Ky's arms
were aching now, and the torches were burning low.

Desperately Ky tried to communicate with his
attackers. 'Listen to me. I am Ky! I come here for
refuge, not to harm you ...'

The Mutants didn't understand, or didn't want to
listen. They kept up their circling, swooping attack,
driving Ky back against the wall. The snapping
claws came closer, closer.

Pressed into her niche in the rock wall, Jo listened
in terror to the sounds of the struggle, sure the Mutants

would destroy Ky and then come looking for her. One of the Mutants, milling about on the fringes of the group, stumbled by the edge of her hiding place, and reached for her with its claws. Jo screamed, dodged frantically past its scaly body and ran—away from the struggle, deeper into the darkness of the mines.

Exhausted, Ky leaned back against the wall, too weary even to raise his guttering torches. The circle of Mutants moved closer ... The great claws reached out ...

Suddenly two torch-carrying figures appeared, falling upon the Mutants with fierce shouts and yells, whirling their blazing branches in arcs of flame. Terrified by this sudden attack from behind, the Mutants fled in panic, disappearing into the darkness. Gathering the last of his strength, Ky helped the Doctor and Varan to drive them away.

Unaware that she'd fled at the moment of rescue, Jo stumbled down the tunnels. Her panic over for the moment, she stopped. It was silly just to go deeper and deeper into the mines. She was about to turn back, when she saw a faint gleam of light, just ahead of her. Curiosity overcame fear, and she moved slowly forward.

The light was streaming from a cleft, a kind of natural door in the tunnel wall. Jo climbed through it, and found herself in fairyland—or so it seemed at first to her dazzled eyes.

She was in an enormous cave, with a high arched roof like a cathedral. It was a cave of light. The rock walls glowed, the ceiling glowed, the strangely shaped rocks scattered around the cave floor glowed, all with a kind of pulsing inner light. The lights blazed in many different colours, producing a kind of jewelled, stained-glass appearance. The effect was startling. Jo found that the pulsing multi-coloured lights were making her dizzy. At least something was ... She took a few faltering steps, and slumped to the ground.

As she lay staring muzzily up at the ever glowing

lights a *thing* appeared. Its huge, lumbering silvery shape moved slowly towards her. The last thing Jo saw before she fainted was a huge round head silhouetted against the glowing light, and two great silver paws reaching out for her ...

Ky glared angrily at Varan, hand on his sword-hilt. 'Why are you here, Varan? Did your Overlord masters send you to kill me?'

'Steady on, old chap,' protested the Doctor. 'He has just helped to save your life.'

Ky and Varan ignored him, glaring at each other like two strange dogs preparing to fight.

'The Marshal betrayed me,' growled Varan at last. 'Now the Overlords are my enemies.'

'At last you see the truth, Varan. We can work together.'

'I want no help from you, Ky, nor do I need it. I shall return to my people, tell them the truth, and lead them in battle against the Overlords.'

Ky turned away. 'And you are the Doctor—the friend of Miss Grant?'

'That's right. And I'd very much like to see her.'

'I hid her in a place of safety when we were attacked. We will go and find her. Why did you come here?'

'To rescue Jo—and to give *you* this!'

The Doctor produced the Time Lord despatch-box and handed it to Ky. Once in Ky's hands the box opened in the same mysterious manner as before. Indeed, from this point it remained a simple box, one which could be opened and closed at will by whoever held it.

Ky looked at the sheaf of ancient scrolls in puzzlement. Varan was scornful. 'Tablets, sketchings—these are not weapons to fight the Overlords.'

Ky looked at the Doctor. 'He is right. How can these things help us?'

'I'm not sure yet. But perhaps these old parchments

may be worth more to you than weapons.'

They studied the scrolls. They were filled with a kind of picture-writing. One particular symbol, a kind of winged man, recurred many times. 'I have seen such signs,' said Ky slowly. 'They are the writings of the Old Ones, the mighty rulers of Solos in the days of our greatness—before Earthmen destroyed our culture. Figures like these are carved on great rocks and old monuments all over Solos. But no one knows what they mean now. No one remembers.'

'They must mean something,' said the Doctor thoughtfully, 'or why would I have been sent here?'

'Why indeed?' said Varan scornfully. 'Come, it is time we were gone.'

'Not until I find Miss Grant,' said the Doctor firmly.

Varan lost patience. 'Fools! Is this the way to defeat the Overlords, to hide down here till we are killed by Mutts? If you will not fight, Varan will.' He turned and strode back towards the mine entrance.

Ky sighed. 'Now he will go and summon his warriors—and for all their valour, they will be wiped out. Swords are no use against the Overlords.'

'Then we must find a better way. But first you must take me to Jo Grant.' As they walked towards the cleft, the Doctor continued, 'Someone on Solos must understand the old writings ...'

Ky paused. 'There was a man called Sondergaard. A man of learning from Earth. He came to Solos to study the remains of our culture. But he quarrelled with the Marshal, threatened to report his wrong-doings to Earth.'

'What happened to him?'

'He disappeared. It was said that the Marshal arranged it—but there was never any proof.' He paused by the cleft. 'This is where I left Miss Grant, Doctor—and she is gone!'

The Marshal was holding a briefing meeting. Stubbs,

Cotton, Professor Jaeger, and an assortment of security guard captains stood listening respectfully as he gestured at a wall-map. 'Basically a simple operation. Satellite surveillance reports that all the people we're looking for are conveniently concentrated in these old mine workings. We surround the place and set off some gas grenades the Professor here has devised. We'll be able to flush all of them out. Mutts, Ky, the girl, the Doctor, the lot!'

He looked round for comments. Stubbs asked, 'Suppose the gas doesn't flush 'em out, sir?'

'Then they'll die down there—and good riddance. All right now, better start setting things up!'

Stubbs, Cotton and the guard captains filed out. Only Jaeger remained. 'I didn't want to interrupt your moment of military glory, Marshal. But things may be less simple than you think. I have some facts and figures you ought to know about.'

The Marshal sighed. 'Well, Jaeger?'

'I've been studying the planetary monitor reports after the storms,' began Jaeger importantly.

'I'm not interested in weather reports, man.'

'Then you should be. There's a rise in temperature after every storm—and no following decrease. Solos is getting hotter and hotter, Marshal. It may soon be too hot for any Earthman to live here.'

'And it may not! Weather's your problem, Jaeger. Mine is wiping out these Mutts.'

'There's a steep rise in the Mutation rate too, Marshal. And a mass migration of Mutants—towards your target area.'

'Excellent!' The Marshal rubbed his big, chubby hands. 'The more the merrier, my dear Jaeger. The more the merrier. This time we'll wipe out the lot of them!'

8

The Trap

Not far from the entrance to the mines, Varan paused suspiciously. He could hear movements coming towards him. Not Solonians. Overlords, crashing through the jungle in their heavy boots.

He saw a squad of Overlord guards moving quickly along the trail, the first of the Marshal's men on their way to surround the mines.

Varan considered. They were directly across his path. But if he waited, more Overlords might come, until there were too many to escape. Better to surprise them now.

He dashed across the trail, and was disappearing into the jungle beyond before the guards had really spotted him. He heard shouted commands to stop, and blaster-bolts sizzled around his head. Varan ducked and weaved and kept running, until the jungle swallowed him up. The guard Captain stared longingly after him. But the Marshal's orders had been clear. He gathered his men and marched them forward to the mines.

Ky and the Doctor, who had been searching separately to cover more ground, came together in the inner chamber. They were tired and dispirited and their torches were burning low. Each could see from the other's face that the search had been unsuccessful. 'We'll just have to carry on,' said the Doctor grimly. '*If* the torches last—and *if* the Mutants don't attack us!'

There was a scuttling sound, and then silence. 'They're watching us all the time,' said Ky softly.

The Doctor nodded. 'Yet they don't attack in the

tunnels—only at the entrance—and in here. As if this area was important to them in some way.'

'I feel it myself,' said Ky unexpectedly. 'A sensation of being drawn here, as if this place is—special. Warm, and safe. A kind of instinctive attraction.'

The Doctor looked hard at him. 'As you say, Ky, it's very strange. We'd better go on with the search.'

They left the chamber and the light of their torches disappeared down the mine shaft. Darkness returned to the chamber for a moment. Then more light appeared. A section of the rock moved away. A huge round silvery head appeared in the opening . . .

Outside the cave the Marshal was deep in conversation with the Captain of the advance guard. 'You're sure it was Varan?'

'Yes, sir. I've often seen him on Skybase.'

'Very well. Say nothing about this to anyone.' The Marshal turned away and raised his voice. 'All right, let's have those grenades over here—and the blast-packs.' Boxes of gas grenades and packets of plastic explosive were carried over to the mine shaft by sweating guards.

Stubbs and Cotton came over to the Marshal and saluted. He looked at them thoughtfully, a curious gleam in his eye. 'Well?'

'Wonder if we ought to search for the Doctor and Miss Grant first,' said Stubbs uneasily.

'Do you now?' said the Marshal smoothly. 'I wonder why.'

Stubbs racked his brains, and Cotton came to his rescue. 'Professor Jaeger needs the Doctor to help him, sir—and the girl's no more than a kid.'

The Marshal seemed to ponder for a moment. 'Very well. It'll take some time to get things set up. You can go down and search. I'll give you fifteen minutes, not a second more.'

Stubbs and Cotton saluted and ran into the mine.

Both felt uneasy—things had gone with suspicious smoothness. They would have felt even more uneasy if they could have seen the smile on the Marshal's lips as he watched them go. He turned to the Captain. 'I want those blast-charges laid at every entrance. Now—get busy!'

Varan stumbled to the edge of the village clearing and looked round in astonishment. The place was deserted. All the huts were empty, the spaces between them littered with cooking pots, clothes, weapons, food, abandoned as if by some retreating army.

Varan made his way to his hut in the centre of the village where the war-gong hung on its wooden framework. At the base of the gong he found an old man huddled face-down on a pile of rags. Varan shook him roughly. 'Awake, old one. Varan, your Chief, has returned. Where are my people?'

The old man began babbling of firestorms in the sky, the sudden wave of Mutations, the compulsion that made everyone leave the village and set off for the abandoned mines. Varan could make little sense of it. 'Summon my council,' he ordered. 'Beat the wargong!'

The old man lurched to his feet and took the heavy wooden gong-stick that hung from the framework. He struck the great gong with his failing strength. Its brazen note hummed through the deserted village. As the old man struck the gong again, Varan looked at his back in horror. Along the spine ran the heavy vertebrae of the Mutant.

The old man beat the gong again and again, but no one came. As the echoing notes died away, Varan cried frantically, 'Why does no one come? Where are my warriors?'

Sadly the old man croaked. 'Your warriors have gone, Varan. It is the way with all of us, old and young.

Those who could walk have gone. To the mines, Varan ... to the mines.'

Varan stared at the back of his own brawny arm. The skin was thickening, becoming scaly. 'No,' he screamed. '*No!*'

He heard a voice inside his head. 'Go to the mines, Varan,' it said. 'Go to the place of sleeping, the place of darkness and light. To the mines, Varan ...'

Desperately Varan fought to hold on to his own personality. 'No! I am Varan!' he shouted. 'I am a warrior. I will not die sleeping. I shall fight!' His voice echoed hollowly through the empty village.

Powerful hand-torches attached to their belts, Stubbs and Cotton ran through the mine shafts calling, 'Doctor! Doctor, Miss Grant, are you there?' Scuttling movements came from all around them, but although they could sense that the mine shafts were teeming with life, no one tried to stop them.

Deeper inside the mine Ky and the Doctor heard the distant voices. 'Overlords!' said Ky. 'We must escape or they will trap us here. Put out the torches or they will see us.'

They ran back to the chamber. The calling voices became louder. 'They're by the entrance,' whispered Ky. 'We must slip past them—or find another exit.'

'Sssh,' whispered the Doctor. 'I thought I heard something.' A low moan came from the edge of the chamber. The Doctor groped his way towards it. He stumbled over something and bent down. 'It's Jo.' he whispered. 'Jo, are you all right?'

Jo opened her eyes. 'Doctor,' she said feebly.

Ky came over. 'But we searched this chamber before —and she wasn't here.'

The cave filled with blinding light and a voice said, 'Ah, there you are!'

'Overlords,' shouted Ky. 'Run, Doctor!'

'Doctor, it's *us*,' shouted Stubbs. 'It's me and Cotton. Did you find Miss Grant?'

'Yes, just a moment ago. It's all right, Ky, these two Overlords are our friends.'

The Marshal stood by the cave entrance, a gun-like directional microphone trained inside. It picked up the babble of explanations and greetings coming from the inner chamber. 'Just as I thought,' muttered the Marshal. 'Traitors, the lot of them. All in league against me.' He took out his communicator. 'All sections. Fire the grenades, then set off the blast charges. I want every entrance sealed.'

Jo had just finished telling the Doctor of her adventures in the glowing cave.

Stubbs said, 'I'd better get back to His Nibs, tell him we've found you all.'

'Steady on,' objected the Doctor. 'I don't particularly want to find myself the Marshal's prisoner again. Nor does Ky.'

'You'll be better off on Skybase than down here, Doctor. The Marshal's mounting a mass attack on the Mutants. It won't worry him a bit if he polishes off you as well!'

Cotton nodded. 'Better hurry, Stubbs, old son. Our time's nearly up. They'll be starting the attack soon.' Stubbs hurried away.

Dazedly, Jo asked, 'Attack? What attack?'

'The Marshal's final solution to the Mutt problem,' said Cotton. 'He's using gas and then explosives.'

'Doesn't he know we're down here?'

'Oh yes, miss. He knows.'

The Marshal counted off the last few seconds of time and shouted, 'Now!' The blast-charges exploded, and a wall of rocks rumbled down, completely covering the entrance to the mine.

Stubbs ran up the tunnel that led to the entrance and stopped short. A great cloud of thick white gas was rolling towards him. Seconds later he heard the rumble of explosions. He turned and ran back.

Inside the cave the Doctor was lost in thought.

'There must be something about this cave,' he muttered. 'A radiation source nearby—probably the cave you wandered into, Jo. But how did you get in—and who carried you out? Let me see those scrolls again, Ky.'

Ky passed over the box, and the Doctor sat studying the scrolls in the light of Cotton's torch.

Stubbs ran back into the chamber. 'The Marshal must have been on to us after all. He's started the attack—early!'

The Doctor helped Jo to her feet. 'We'd better get out of here.'

'We can't,' said Cotton desperately. 'He's sealed off the exit as well!'

For a moment they looked at each other, baffled. Then Jo said, 'Look—over there!'

On the far side of the chamber a silvery-suited figure was standing. 'That's the thing I saw in the cave,' whispered Jo. The figure beckoned to them, and began moving away.

'Come on,' said the Doctor. 'I *think* it's friendly.' He coughed as gas began seeping into the chamber. 'We've got to follow it anyway, whatever it is.'

The strange silver figure led them deeper and deeper into the mines, stopping from time to time to make sure they were following. As they moved along, they heard low rumblings from all around.

'The Marshal's making sure of things this time,' said Stubbs. 'That's the other exits.'

'Was the other exits,' corrected Cotton.

There was another rumble. 'If he keeps that up

71

the whole mountain will come down,' muttered Stubbs.

The suited figure led them down a side-gallery, which ended in a heavy metal door. It touched a control and the door slid back, revealing light beyond. With another beckoning gesture, the figure moved through the door. They all followed. The Doctor scratched curiously at the metal as he went through. It felt strangely soft, like lead. 'Radiation,' he thought, and went through the door after the others. It slid closed behind him.

They found themselves in a rock-walled cave which had been lovingly converted into a primitive laboratory. It looked rather like an up to date enchanter's cave, modern equipment all mixed up with native pots and jars of flowering herbs. The shape was now revealed to be someone wearing a radiation-suit; the giant domed head was a protective helmet. They watched in fascination as the figure unfastened the clips on the helmet and lifted it off. They saw a brown, wrinkled, kindly face, chiefly remarkable for an almost complete absence of hair. Jo was relieved to see that their host was at least human. He smiled shyly at them and said softly, 'Welcome! You must not be afraid. My name is . . .'

The Doctor was already moving forward, his hand outstretched. 'How do you do?' he said politely. 'Professor Sondergaard, I presume?'

9

The Fugitive

The Marshal surveyed the rock-filled mine entrance with satisfaction, and turned to the guard Captain. 'I am now returning to Skybase. I want every exit sealed, you understand. Every exit!'

Nervously the Captain said, 'That's impossible, sir. We've covered the main exits, but these galleries run on for miles. We'd need an army to cover them all.'

The Marshal brooded. 'All right. Give the gas time to clear, then take a patrol down. You might be able to mop up one or two survivors.'

Jamming his oxy-mask in place, and summoning his escort, the Marshal set off back through the jungle.

Sondergaard bustled about the laboratory, which was also his home. He provided a simple meal for his guests, water, fruits, a little native bread. It wasn't much, but they all ate and drank hungrily. To Jo it seemed a feast. While they ate, Sondergaard chattered continuously. The effect of company after so many years of solitude had suddenly gone to his head. 'Naturally there *is* radiation, after all this was once a thaesium mine. But it is not dangerous, unless you approach the unstable area—the one where I found you, young lady.'

Jo swallowed a mouthful of peach-like fruit and said, 'It was you I saw then? You brought me out?'

'I was so surprised that I didn't know what to do. I couldn't leave you there. I took you to where your friends would find you.'

Jo smiled her thanks and went on eating.

Ky looked curiously at the brown-faced little man.

73

'We thought you had died long ago, Professor.'

'And all the time I was a fugitive in the mines—like your Mutants. They were my only friends.'

Jo looked up. 'The Mutants attacked us, tried to kill us—didn't they, Ky?'

Sondergaard shrugged. 'There are more of them now, many more. As their numbers increase, so does their aggressiveness.'

'Who made them aggressive?' said Ky indignantly. 'The Overlords, by hunting them like animals.' He looked suspiciously at Sondergaard. '*Why* have you hidden in the caves all this time? Do you experiment on my people?'

'Do you think I live in these conditions from choice, young man?' asked Sondergaard mildly. 'I was young and ambitious when I came to Solos. I hoped to make great discoveries. My first was that Solos was becoming a slave planet. I sent a secret report to Earth Council. The Marshal intercepted it. I was lucky to escape with my life. I fled to the shelter of these caves. I have been here ever since.'

The Doctor looked round the improvised laboratory. 'But you *have* continued with your research?'

'As best I could. As you see, my equipment is primitive. If it were not for the Mutants I would never have survived here.'

'The Mutants help you?' said Ky. 'You can communicate with them?'

'After a fashion. Once they stole food for me and clothing. We were all outcasts, we helped each other. But now they have changed.' Sondergaard shook his head mournfully. 'Strange things are happening on Solos. Not just to the people, but to the soil, the plants, the atmosphere ... the planet itself is changing ...'

The Doctor leaned forward. 'Is it because of Jaeger's experiments with the atmosphere, the changing of the weather?'

Sondergaard nodded solemnly. 'My belief is this

74

'... At first the changes were natural. But Jaeger's experiments *accelerated* them—to the point where things are going seriously wrong.'

The Doctor began pacing about the laboratory. 'But why was *I* sent here?' he demanded. 'And what have those scrolls to do with it all?'

He took the box from Ky and showed the scrolls to Sondergaard, who studied them absorbedly. 'This is wonderful, Doctor. Marvellous! Where did you get them? I have seen such signs as these carved on the oldest monuments of Solos.'

'Professor Sondergaard, please! Can you *read* them?'

'I can most certainly try. I have approximate translations for many of the main symbols. This is the Solonian book of Genesis, Doctor. The story of how Solonian civilisation began——'

There was a sudden explosion. It shook the cave and debris was shaken from the ceiling, clattering over Sondergaard's instruments.

'Unless we get a move on, it'll be the story of how it ended,' said the Doctor ruefully.

Stubbs drew the Doctor aside. 'That wasn't just a blast-charge, Doctor. I reckon the Marshal's explosions have weakened the whole mountain. The tunnels are falling in. We could all be trapped.'

The Doctor thought hard. 'Professor Sondergaard, is there an exit the Marshal might have missed? Somewhere secret?'

Sondergaard looked up from the scrolls. 'There is one—a disused access shaft. It surfaces near one of the native villages.'

Ky said, 'Varan's village is the nearest to here.'

The Doctor stood up. 'Stubbs, you and Cotton take Ky and Miss Grant to safety.'

Jo looked worriedly at him. 'What about you, Doctor?'

'The key to everything is in this room. The scrolls, Professor Sondergaard's records, his knowledge of the Solonian language. I must find the answers I need.'

'But you heard what Stubbs said, the mountain's falling in!'

'Nonsense. It takes more than a day for a mountain to fall down. We'll get out in time.'

Jo knew the Doctor was talking with a confidence he didn't feel.

Stubbs stood impatiently by the door. 'Come on, Miss Grant, please.'

Sondergaard opened the metal door for them. 'You will find the opening to the access-shaft at the end of the tunnel, to your left. It is very small, but you will be able to squeeze through. Take always the path leading upwards!'

He ushered them out of the door, closed it, and went eagerly back to the scrolls. 'Now then, Doctor, this particular sign here is the Solonian symbol for life ...'

Stubbs and Cotton in the lead, Jo and Ky close behind, the little party moved along the tunnel. Their only encounter was with a panic-stricken Mutant. More frightened than they were, it scuttled away into the darkness.

Stubbs stopped by a narrow opening in the wall. 'Well this is it, I reckon.' They scrambled inside and began their long and difficult journey to the surface.

The Doctor and Sondergaard worked on the scrolls for a very long time, ignoring the sinister rumbles from overhead. The Doctor ran impatient fingers through his hair. 'I can't understand why the same symbols crop up so often ...'

Sondergaard nodded his sympathy. 'Some kind of cycle, perhaps, Doctor? Or a chemical process ...'

'But what process repeats itself endlessly?'

'Only life itself,' said Sondergaard slowly. 'Life in some form will always go on.'

Another explosion nearby showered them with debris. The Doctor looked up rather apprehensively. 'Let us hope so, Professor Sondergaard. Let us hope so!'

After an age of tortuous wriggling upwards, the little tunnel led the group into another mine gallery. 'We must be very near the surface now,' whispered Stubbs.

They froze at the sound of booted footsteps.

Peering from the tunnel they saw a security guard moving towards them. Stubbs looked meaningfully at Ky and then stepped boldly out into the gallery. 'All right, mate, it's nothing to worry about, it's only me. You remember old Stubbsy.'

So calm and confident was his tone that it took the guard a moment too long to remember that old Stubbsy was now proclaimed an outlaw. As he raised his blaster Ky charged him from one side and clubbed him down.

'There'll be more of 'em,' whispered Stubbs. 'We'd better get moving.'

They began making for the light at the end of the tunnel.

'It's a code,' said the Doctor despairingly. Then suddenly he jumped up. 'No it isn't—it's a *calendar*! Eureka!' He pointed to the scroll they were studying. 'You see—Spring, Summer, Autumn, Winter.' He beamed triumphantly at Sondergaard.

'But Solos has no seasons, Doctor. It does not tilt on its axis relative to its sun.'

The Doctor studied another scroll. 'It doesn't tilt, my dear Sondergaard, it moves closer. These ellipses are the orbits.'

Sondergaard looked up excitedly. 'And if Solos takes

two thousand years to go round its sun in this fashion ...'

'Then the seasons must be five hundred years long!' concluded the Doctor triumphantly. 'Solos is moving from Spring into its long, long Summer.'

Once he had worked out the first clue, the Doctor's mind worked at tremendous speed. He raced through the scrolls making copious notes, leaving the astonished Sondergaard far behind. Suddenly the Doctor leaped to his feet. 'You see these sun-like symbols here? Radiation, my dear chap. A vital clue. Somehow radiation is part of the puzzle. You must take me to the place where you found Jo.'

'I have only one protective suit. If you spend too much time in there you will collapse—any man would.'

The Doctor smiled. 'Any human would, perhaps,' he said cheerfully. 'Come along now, Professor, lead the way!'

Although this particular entrance had not been sealed by the Marshal's bombs, it had partially fallen in over years of disuse. The last stage of the journey was a scramble up an almost vertical rock face, all that was left of a long-vanished staircase. Exhausted, the little group scrambled up the loose and uneven rocks. A gleam of daylight came through the vines that covered the mouth of the shaft. Ky and Cotton took the lead in the climb. Jo was next and Stubbs came last.

Jo glanced upwards to see if the top was getting any nearer—and suddenly saw a fierce helmeted face glaring down at her. She stopped climbing with a gasp. Cotton looked down at her. 'What's the matter?'

'There was someone up there.'

Cotton looked. 'No one there now, miss.'

'Well, there *was* someone there. He was wearing a winged helmet.'

'A warrior,' said Ky. 'We are near Varan's village.

His people will be in an angry mood!'

Cotton drew his blaster. He scrambled past Ky and over the edge of the shaft. 'Anything?' called Stubbs.

Cotton's head appeared over the edge. 'No one in sight.'

'Right, up we go then!'

Ky, Jo and finally Stubbs himself scrambled out of the mine shaft to join Cotton. All except Ky adjusted their oxy-masks as they looked around the misty jungle.

Now it was Ky who took the lead. 'We'd better make for Varan's village,' he said. 'It isn't far away—and besides, it's the only place to go.'

They set off through the jungle.

Varan held court in the chieftain's hut. His entourage was reduced to the handful of warriors he had been able to produce from his own village and the others nearby. Like Varan himself all wore ceremonial armour and fierce winged helmets. Varan looked round proudly. 'We few are all that are left. We are warriors still. Shall we crawl into darkness to die? Or shall we fight one last time, and die as warriors?'

A growl of approval went round the little group. Another warrior ran into the hut. He too was armoured and helmeted. 'Overlords, Varan. They climb up from the place of darkness.'

Varan stood up, reaching for his sword. 'Make ready!'

Ky, Stubbs, Cotton and Jo moved cautiously through the apparently deserted village, peering into the empty huts. They reached the chief's hut in the centre, with the war-gong hanging outside. Suddenly Varan appeared in the doorway, magnificent in his ornately decorated armour and winged helmet, sword in hand. 'Now!' he bellowed, and more armed warriors appeared all around them. They were surrounded.

Stubbs raised his blaster, and moved back to back with Cotton. 'I reckon there's only about half-a-dozen all told,' he said quietly. 'We can handle them.'

Although Varan was his enemy, Ky was unable to see fellow Solonians shot down. 'No, don't shoot,' he shouted. 'We should all be on the same side.'

Instinctively Stubbs and Cotton glanced towards him. The brief diversion was enough for Varan. He reached out and grabbed Jo by one arm, twisting her round so she stood in front of him, his sword at her throat. 'Lay down your weapons, Overlords,' he shouted, 'or the girl dies—now!'

10

The Crystal

The Doctor stood by the entrance to the radiation cave, Sondergaard at his side. Both were entranced by the glowing multi-coloured beauty around them. It was like being in the heart of an enormous diamond.

'It's magnificent,' murmured the Doctor. 'Like some great cathedral.' He peered into the depths of the cave. 'There seems to be a kind of centre—a focal point. Let's make for that.'

They moved slowly forward, and as they advanced, the interplay of multi-coloured lights became ever more dazzling. The Doctor had a far greater degree of mental control than any human being, but he was beginning to feel overpowered by the dazzling radiance. Sondergaard was having an even harder time. He staggered and fell, his hands shielding the face-plate of his helmet. The Doctor heard his muffled voice. 'I can't ... go on. You'll have to leave me, Doctor.'

The Doctor hesitated for a moment, then forged ahead. After a lengthy journey through overwhelming brightness, he found himself gazing into a transparent globe, apparently the source of all the energy that filled the cave. Inside the globe was a face, calm, radiant, beautiful. It seemed to smile out at him. Below the globe was a glowing crystal, and somehow the Doctor knew that this was what he had come to find. He reached forward and picked it up. As the Doctor took the crystal the face in the globe seemed to smile in approval. Then it vanished, as the globe itself shivered into the finest dust.

Crystal in hand, the Doctor turned and made his way back across the cave. He paused by the unconscious body of Sondergaard, hoisting it onto his shoulder. Then, crystal in his hand and the body of Sondergaard a dead weight across his back, the Doctor made his way out of the cave.

Hands bound securely behind them, Stubbs, Cotton, Ky and Jo were prisoners in Varan's hut. Once Varan had seized Jo the struggle was over. Stubbs and Cotton had been forced to throw down their weapons. It was that or take a chance that Varan was bluffing— and Jo, for one, was very glad they hadn't risked it.

Magnificent in his battle armour, Varan stood over them. 'You will suffer as I have suffered, Overlords.' He kicked Ky in the ribs, 'And you, renegade, will die!'

'You're a fool, Varan,' gasped Ky. 'Attack Skybase and you'll lose the pitiful handful of warriors you have left.'

Varan stripped the gauntlet from his left hand and showed the mutating insect-claw. 'What have I left to fear? Revenge is all that is left to me!'

'You cannot hope to enter Skybase, much less destroy it ...'

Varan laughed. 'You forget, Ky, we have these Overlords now.' He gestured towards Stubbs and Cotton who looked impassively back at him. 'We have their weapons, and the young female to be our shield.' He laughed again. 'You will all die in a good cause, renegade. The cause of Varan's revenge.'

The Marshal stormed into the laboratory and glared at Jaeger, who sat hunched on a lab stool still trying to work out the way the Doctor's particle reversal set-up had been *supposed* to work. 'Are the ionisation rockets ready for the bombardment?'

Jaeger spoke reprovingly. 'Marshal, this is not a war, you know. It is a scientific experiment to show that population control can be affected by atmospheric means ...'

The Marshal sneered. 'Experiments, population control ... all so much jargon, Jaeger. This *is* war—and don't you forget it! How soon can you get the countdown started?'

Jaeger stared indignantly at him. 'Are you aware, Marshal, just how long it takes to check out an orbital rocket? Particularly the kind of antiquated hardware with which you expect me to work?'

'You've got the Skybase engineers to help you.'

Jaeger sniffed. 'They've deteriorated almost as much as the rockets.'

'Excuses, Jaeger, excuses!' roared the Marshal. His communicator bleeped. 'Well?'

'Message from deep space,' said the infuriatingly smug voice of the computer. 'Message reads "Unscheduled *Hyperion* Space-shuttle now on course Solos. Arrival time 22.29. Earth Council Investigator on board." Message ends.'

The Marshal hammered his fist on a bench, rattling every piece of equipment in the place. '*Blast* Earth Council. Who do they think they are? Investigator indeed. What's he going to investigate?'

'Your regime should give him plenty of scope,' said Jaeger waspishly.

The Marshal grabbed Jaeger by the collar and lifted him off his feet. 'If I didn't need you, Jaeger ...' He shook the tubby scientist until the teeth rattled in his head.

'Now listen,' he said softly. 'By the time the Investigator arrives, it will all be over. Your experiments will have been successfully concluded, the Mutts will have been eliminated, and the air on Solos will be breathable for humans. Understand?'

'But the rockets,' gasped Jaeger. 'They're only half ready. I haven't even worked out my experimental conclusions fully ...'

The Marshal dropped Jaeger, and dusted his palms

together. There was a mad glint in his eyes. 'Either the rockets go, or you go, my dear Professor,' he said sinisterly, and struck a Napoleonic pose. 'I intend to meet the Investigator, face to face on the soil of Solos—without masks! I will present him with a new planet for humanity. What will become of his petty criticisms then?'

The new duty guards at the Solos transfer station were surprised to see Stubbs and Cotton strolling casually towards them along the corridor. They were even more surprised when Varan's warriors pulled them down from behind.

Varan came forward and looked down at the unconscious guards. 'You did well, Overlords. Now the way to Skybase lies open to us.'

Stubbs spoke patiently, like someone talking to an obstinate child. 'Varan, you don't stand a chance.'

'We are ready to die,' said Varan simply. 'That is why we have come.'

'What good will that do?' protested Jo. 'I'm sure the Doctor will be able to help you.'

Varan held up his mutated hand. 'There is no cure for *this*! Now, into the transfer cubicles, all of you.'

The Doctor was studying the crystal from the cave under Sondergaard's microscope. Beside him, Sondergaard lay resting on a couch. Once away from the glowing cave he had recovered rapidly, and was now almost his old self. The Doctor looked up from the microscope, studying one of the scrolls. 'That's it, right enough. The Solonians are *meant* to mutate. It's part of their natural evolution. They change as their environment changes, every five hundred years. A life cycle unique in the universe. Now, thanks to the Marshal, it's threatened with extinction.'

Sondergaard said eagerly, 'So the Mutations are not a sickness?'

'Certainly not. Rather, they are a metamorphosis ... an adaptive change. The Mutants are only a kind of halfway stage.'

'So we have yet to see the final metamorphosis?'

The Doctor nodded. 'The tablets led us to the crystal—and the crystal was left by the Old Ones. Somehow I feel it must play a vital part in correcting what has gone wrong. But how?'

'Maybe the cellular change is affected in some way by the crystal?'

'Perhaps so. I need to analyse the crystal, to discover its proper function.'

Sondergaard sighed. 'As you see, Doctor, my equipment here is far too primitive for crystallography. There is only one place that such work could be done.'

The Doctor nodded. 'Jaeger's laboratory,' he said slowly. 'On Skybase ...'

Jo, Cotton, Stubbs and Ky appeared in the transfer cubicles on Skybase. Varan was waiting for them, and his warriors brought up the rear.

Herding their captives before them as a living shield, Varan and his warriors moved along the corridor.

A voice spoke out of the air. 'All sectors cleared, all systems green and go on countdown. Forty-seven seconds ... forty-five and counting ...'

In Jaeger's laboratory, the Marshal and Jaeger stood listening to the countdown. The Marshal looked exultant, Jaeger looked terrified. 'Marshal, this is stupid,' he began. 'I can take no responsibility ...'

The Marshal waved him to silence as a new message came over the speaker. 'Emergency, emergency, unauthorised personnel detected by monitor cameras in transfer section. Countdown held.'

The Marshal snatched up his communicator. 'This is the Marshal. Continue countdown. Security squad to Transfer Section immediately.' He rushed to the door, and paused to snarl at Jaeger. 'Nothing is going to stop this countdown, *nothing!*'

Moving along the corridor, Jo heard the calm voice cut off for a moment and then continue. 'Twenty-one. Twenty seconds and counting ...'

'What's all that about?' she whispered.

Stubbs shrugged. 'Must be one of Jaeger's experiments. He's shot off rockets before.'

'Silence,' hissed Varan.

Stubbs came to a sudden halt. His ears had caught an all-too-familiar sound—the click of a blaster being cocked. He shoved Jo, Ky and Cotton to the floor. 'Get down, quick!'

As they dropped, the Marshal and his guards appeared at one end of the corridor. More guards at the other. Caught in a deadly cross-fire, Varan's warriors were blasted down. Their bodies fell almost on top of Jo and the others, acting as a shield.

At the end of the burst of firing, only Varan was still on his feet, his warriors dead all around him. Wounded, he raised his sword for a final charge—and the Marshal blasted it from his hand.

Varan staggered and reeled back. The Marshal marched slowly towards him, and Varan slumped back against the corridor wall.

Raising his blaster the Marshal fired again and again, with cold-blooded determination. The energy-bolts slammed Varan's already dead body against the wall. The Marshal went on blasting so wildly that his next shots missed the falling Varan and punched a hole in the wall of Skybase itself. In his rage the Marshal had forgotten that this was an outer wall.

With a terrifying shriek of escaping air, Varan's body was snatched through the gaping hole and out into space.

Obliviously the computer completed its countdown: '... Two, one, zero.'

There was a deafening roar and the unseen rockets streaked away from Skybase. But the Marshal was in no condition to enjoy this long-awaited moment. Like the others, he was being slowly sucked towards the gaping hole through which Varan had disappeared ...

11

Condemned

Jo was the nearest to the hole. She was saved by Ky, who made a desperate lunge to grab her arm. Cotton grabbed hold of Ky, and Stubbs grabbed Cotton. Lying flat on the floor they formed a human chain ... but despite all their efforts, they were being sucked closer to the hole. So too was the Marshal. No one had bothered to grab hold of him, and he was left to struggle against the pressure alone.

Over the howl of escaping air they heard the calm voice of the computer. 'Emergency in Section Three. De-pressurise and isolate.'

Cotton shouted, 'The pressure will ease in a minute. When that happens we've got to get through that door along there, before the air goes completely ...'

Jo felt the drag of the hole begin to lessen. Helped by Ky, she was able to struggle to her feet. Like people fighting against a gale they forced themselves along the wall and through the connecting door. The Marshal, in a final burst of terrified strength, managed to tumble through after them. Cotton slammed the door and they struggled to their feet, gasping for breath. Stubbs helped Jo to her feet. 'You all right, Miss Grant?'

'I think so,' gasped Jo. 'You saved my life, all of you ...'

'Very touching,' sneered a familiar voice. The Marshal had recovered too, and he was covering them with his blaster.

'Guards!' he bellowed, and they heard booted feet running along the corridor. Jo sighed. They were the Marshal's prisoners again ... but at least they were alive.

* * *

The Doctor and Sondergaard emerged from the caves by the exit that Jo and the others had used. They were greeted by a piercing shriek, and a tremendous explosion in the jungle close by. They flung themselves to the ground.

Sondergaard raised his voice above the noise. 'What's happening, Doctor?'

'Rockets!' shouted the Doctor. 'That fool Jaeger is actually bombarding the planet with rockets!'

They pressed themselves to the ground. There were more whistling shrieks, and more explosions, though none as near as the first one. At last the deafening noises stopped. The Doctor stood up. 'The fireworks seem to be over for the moment. Let's try to catch up with the others.'

A fairly short trip through the jungle brought them to the outskirts of Varan's village. Everything around them was silent. Not far away, part of the jungle was on fire. They caught glimpses of black smoke drifting above the dense trees.

The Doctor paused on a hill just above the village and fished out a pocket-telescope. He studied the village carefully—it was utterly deserted. 'No sign of them—or of Varan.' The Doctor considered for a moment. 'Varan said he planned to attack Skybase. If the others met him as he was setting off, he might well have taken them along, as hostages or decoys.' He put the telescope away. 'Professor Sondergaard, I think we'd better head for the transfer station.'

There was a heavy metal rail set into the wall of the Marshal's office. It had been used for securing prisoners before, and now Jo, Ky, Stubbs and Cotton were fastened to it, their hands pressed one each side of the rail behind their backs and handcuffed together. They stood in an awkward, uncomfortable line, as the Marshal passed before them, like someone reviewing a parade.

'Splendid,' he said happily. 'This time, as you see, we are taking no chances.'

A guard Captain came into the room and saluted, trying to ignore the reproachful stares from Stubbs and Cotton. 'Firing party ready, sir.'

Jo couldn't believe her ears. 'Firing party?'

The Marshal beamed. 'Didn't I tell you? You've all been condemned to summary execution.'

'What about a trial?'

'Certainly, my dear.' The Marshal walked along the line of prisoners once more. 'Stubbs, treason. Cotton, treason. Ky, conspiracy, sabotage, terrorism.' Ky smiled ironically. The Marshal came to a halt before Jo and sighed. 'And you, Miss Grant—such a pity.'

'She had nothing to do with it,' shouted Ky.

The Marshal ignored him. 'Bring in the firing squad.'

Four particularly thuggish-looking guards marched into the office. Stubbs and Cotton sighed despairingly at the sight of them These were the Marshal's pet 'gorillas', too stupid to be trusted with any authority, but loyal enough to obey any order, no matter how brutal.

The Marshal shouted. 'Squad forward. At the ready!'

The four thugs lined up, raising their blasters.

'The justice of the Overlords,' said Ky scornfully.

'Exactly,' said the Marshal. 'By the way, don't worry about the wall, it's specially reinforced.'

Ky strained defiantly at his chains. 'You'll never win, Marshal,' he shouted. 'So long as one of my people remains, you will never be safe. My death is unimportant—there will be others after me ...'

The Marshal smiled benignly. 'Always the speech-maker, Ky. But I'm afraid you're wrong. There will be no one after you. We're making sure of that.' He turned to the squad of guards. 'Ready. Aim!' He paused, savouring the moment.

Jo stared at the row of blaster-nozzles. It was all so sudden, so unbelievable, that she wasn't even frightened. It was like being trapped in some weird nightmare, from which you knew you would soon awake. Ky was straining against the handcuffs in a last attempt to get his hands on the Marshal. Stubbs and Cotton stood to a kind of attention, faces blank. She saw the Marshal open his mouth to speak—then Jaeger burst into the room. He carried rolls of computer print-out in his hands, and he was in a state of hysterical rage.

'Ruined,' he sobbed. 'The whole operation has been ruined, Marshal—thanks to your stupid premature ...'

The Marshal waved him away. 'Later, Jaeger, I'm a little busy.'

Jaeger took in the squad of guards, the line of chained prisoners. He was irritated rather than horrified. 'Tell all these people to get out. This is more important.'

'Jaeger, I warn you ...'

Sheer rage had given Jaeger courage. 'Marshal, do you want to know about the disaster on Solos—or are you too busy playing soldiers?'

The Marshal choked with rage—then suddenly his face cleared. What better way to prolong the suffering of his prisoners than another agonising delay? He dismissed the guards. 'Wait outside. I'll be needing you again very soon!' He turned to his prisoners. 'You'll forgive a short postponement?' The guards stamped out. 'Well, Jaeger?'

The scientist's voice was shaking with rage. He waved the print-outs. 'Here are the figures. They add up to total failure. Every one of the ionisation rocket malfunctioned in one way or another. They explod on the planet, not in the atmosphere. If only y waited.'

The Marshal had no time for regrets. 'V didn't. So what's happened, Jaeger?'

'The atmosphere is unaffected. It is the

91

the planet that has been contaminated. You have made yourself master of a desert, Marshal. Once those ionisation crystals have taken full effect, no one will be able to set foot on Solos for centuries ...'

'Shut up, Jaeger!'

Jaeger was beside himself. He waved scornfully at the row of chained prisoners, who had been listening to his tirade in fascination. 'As for this display of megalomania—how do you hope to conceal that from the Investigator? They're not all as loyal as those morons outside, you know. Someone will talk, to save his own skin.'

The Marshal moved menacingly towards Jaeger, his tiny eyes glinting with anger, the great hands reaching out. 'Someone like you, Jaeger?' He looked as if he was about to throttle Jaeger on the spot.

Jo decided it was time she intervened. 'You ought to listen to him,' she shouted. 'He's right, someone *will* talk.'

The Marshal swung round on her. 'Not if I dispose of you all first.'

Now Stubbs joined in. 'Can't dispose of all Skybase. You've got a problem, Marshal—no one wants to stay here—except you.'

'The men will obey my orders.'

'Will they? There's more than me and Cotton who don't like what's been going on.'

Jo continued the attack. 'The Investigator will find out *everything* ... the Administrator murdered, the native leaders missing, the planet contaminated ...'

'And suppose the Investigator never arrives?'

'Shoot down an Earth spaceship, Marshal?' jeered Stubbs. 'You'd never dare. And even if you tried, how reliable are your rockets? Or your early warning systems? The Doctor and Miss Grant landed on Skybase without being detected.'

Harried from all sides like a hunted bear, the Marshal snarled, 'The Doctor! Always the Doctor!'

'No one else can help you,' said Jo defiantly. She

decided to bluff. 'We know all about the Investigator. He's coming to investigate the Doctor's findings.'

'And where is your precious Doctor?'

Jo managed a confident smile. 'He's on Solos, Marshal, with Professor Sondergaard. Both of them are very much alive!'

The Doctor and Sondergaard were still struggling through the jungle. Although Sondergaard was using a stolen oxy-mask, he was breathing with some difficulty, and moving very slowly. It was some time since he had made a long journey on the surface of the planet.

The Doctor helped him along as best he could, but they had to make frequent stops so Sondergaard could rest.

They came to a charred area of jungle, close to the point where one of the rockets had crashed. Even beyond the flame-scorched area, there seemed something strange about the vegetation. The Doctor plucked a kind of broad palm-leaf. Apparently quite unharmed, it crumbled away to dust in his hands.

Sondergaard had been watching the Doctor. 'What's happening?'

'Jaeger's rockets failed to explode in space. They crashed on the planet, and now the ionisation crystals are spreading contamination on the surface. If it isn't stopped . . .' The Doctor shook his head. 'We must get to Skybase.'

Sondergaard laid a hand on the Doctor's arm. 'Leave me here, Doctor.'

'My dear chap, I wouldn't dream of it . . .'

'You must. I'm exhausted. I will never make it to Skybase. I shall rest here for a while, then return to my caves. The subsidence has almost ended now, I'll be safe there.' The Doctor was about to protest again but Sondergaard held up his hand. 'Now go, please. You have important work to do.'

The Doctor knew Sondergaard was right. Gently he said, 'Take care, Professor. We will meet again very soon.' He turned and disappeared into the jungle.

The Marshal bustled back into his office, Jaeger at his heels. 'It seems you were right. Miss Grant. The Doctor *is* alive. One of our surveillance satellites has spotted him on Solos. We even know where he *is*.'

'Then why don't you arrest him?'

'We shall, Miss Grant. It seems we need the Doctor!'

'It's big of you to admit it. Why?'

Jaeger came forward. 'There is a technique known as particle reversal, Miss Grant. We wish to use the Doctor's knowledge to, er, sweep the dust under the carpet, before the Investigator arrives.'

'And suppose the Doctor refuses to co-operate?'

'He will co-operate, Miss Grant,' said the Marshal confidently. 'You and your friends are the guarantee of that! I shall now return to Solos, and supervise the Doctor's capture.'

Without Sondergaard to slow him down, the Doctor was able to move very swiftly through the misty jungles. Even in the atmosphere of Solos his amazing constitution was capable of tremendous efforts in time of need. Before long he was approaching the transfer station. As the building appeared through the jungle, the Doctor came to a sudden halt. Black-uniformed men were pouring out of it, supervised by a bulky, unmistakable figure. One of the Marshal's hunting parties ... and it was easy to guess who they were hunting. The Doctor dropped to the ground and wriggled towards the edge of the clearing in which the building stood. Soon he was close enough to hear the Marshal's voice. 'Keep the pressure on. Once you've spotted him, drive him towards me. Remember, I want him in one piece!'

The guards spread out in a long line, and began moving forward, the Marshal following some distance behind. The Doctor made a swift calculation. It seemed likely that the guard at the nearest end of the line would just miss him. The Doctor moved into a crouch, waiting. Sure enough he heard the sound of heavy boots coming nearer and nearer ... When it seemed they had passed him by, the Doctor leaped to his feet and ran for the transfer station.

Unfortunately, he had miscalculated. One extra guard had arrived late and tagged himself on to the line. He was a hulking brute of a man, one of the Marshal's gorillas, and the Doctor cannoned straight into him. Although he was very stupid, the guard was also very strong. He seized the Doctor in a bear-hug and bellowed, 'He's here. I've got him!' The Doctor felt as if his ribs were going to crack. He could hear excited shouts, and the sound of people running towards him ...

The Message

Once he had recovered from his surprise, it didn't take the Doctor long to deal with his captor. He wriggled his lean body, twisted, found a grip on his opponent's thick wrist, bent double and *heaved*. The astonished guard found himself flipped into a somersault that landed him on the ground, head-first. The Doctor disentangled himself and ran for the transfer station.

The guard's shouts had attracted some of the others, and the Doctor was spotted. 'There he is,' one shouted. 'After him!'

A little way off in the jungle, the Marshal realised that his quarry had somehow managed to get behind him. Shuddering at the thought of the Doctor loose on Skybase, he turned and lumbered back towards the transfer station.

The Doctor was inside by now, running through the concrete corridor with guards at his heels. He reached the transfer cubicles, dashed inside one—and vanished with a cheery wave just as the guards came in sight.

The Marshal panted up and saw from the guards' faces that the Doctor had escaped them. 'Don't just stand there, you fools,' he bellowed. 'Get after him!' There was a sudden scramble for the cubicles.

The Doctor materialised in the cubicle on Skybase and set off down the corridor. There was no one about, and he smiled as he realised that the Marshal and all available guards were down on Solos hunting him. They'd soon be back though.

Meanwhile the Marshal's office was presumably empty. The Doctor decided to take a look, in the hope of discovering some incriminating evidence that would give him a lever to use on the Marshal.

He reached the office without being seen—and was astonished to find his four friends strung up like chickens on the Marshal's wall-rail. He raised a finger to his lips for silence, tip-toed across the room to Jo, produced his sonic screwdriver, and started to work on her handcuffs.

Jo gave a silent, delighted grin. How like the Doctor to pop up out of nowhere, just when everything seemed hopeless! But her joy was premature. The Doctor had barely started work when something clattered onto the floor. It was a metal key. They all looked up.

Flanked by his guards, the Marshal stood in the doorway. 'Use the key, Doctor,' he purred. 'But remember what might happen to Miss Grant and the others if you do!' The blasters of the guards were trained on the helpless prisoners.

The Doctor picked up the key. He straightened up, and tossed it on the Marshal's desk. 'All right, what do you want?'

'Jaeger has made a hash of his experiments. He seems to think you can help him make the planet habitable again.'

'And if I do?'

'You and your friends will go on living,' said the Marshal simply. 'You can guess what will happen to them and to you, if you don't co-operate. Why delay, Doctor? After all, it's not just their lives. A whole planet is at stake.'

The Doctor accepted defeat—for the moment. 'Very well, I'll do what I can to clean up after you.'

'Splendid. Oh, and there's one other thing. Your superior, the Investigator, is arriving shortly.'

'My superior?' The Doctor didn't realise that the Marshal was now convinced he was some kind of agent for Earth Council.

Ignoring the Doctor's interruption the Marshal continued, 'I want to make sure my reform will meet with his approval. *You* will confirm the necessity of firm measures. After all, outbreaks of plague and rebellion must be controlled—don't you agree, Doctor?'

The Doctor looked at the Marshal in disbelief. Did the man really think he could still get away with this string of monstrous crimes? 'You're insane,' he said quietly.

The Marshal smiled. 'Only if I lose, Doctor. Only if I lose.'

The Doctor stood listening to Jaeger's account of the state of affairs on Solos. 'Well, you have made a hash of things, haven't you?' he said as he studied a planetary map which showed the areas of contagion.

'It was not my decision, Doctor.'

'No, no, you were just obeying orders. A common excuse. Now then, I shall need a powerful maser-beam.'

Jaeger looked puzzled. 'There's only one maser on Skybase—the one we use in the transfer system. You can scarcely use that ...'

'We've got to. We shall train it on the affected areas like a searchlight and burn out the contagion. It's going to leave a few bald patches—but it's the best we can do.'

Jaeger was impressed, but still very worried. 'It's a brilliant plan, Doctor, and so simple. But it means isolating Skybase. I shall have to get the Marshal's authority.'

'Then stop dilly-dallying and get it, Jaeger. This experiment is going to be extremely dangerous. If we don't rig up an efficient control-mechanism, we could blow up the whole of Skybase!'

The guard in charge of the prisoners prowled restlessly round the room. He found their cold stares unnerving, and wished the Marshal would return. He gave the prisoners a last check, then moved over to wait by the door.

Once he had moved away, Jo jingled her handcuffs a little to attract the attention of Ky and the others. By craning round they were able to see that her handcuffs were fractionally open.

The Doctor's work with the sonic screwdriver hadn't been entirely in vain. Jo's wrists were particularly small, and she had been working at the loosened handcuff for some time. With a final painful wrench that tore her skin, her hand came free.

Ky nodded meaningfully towards the guard, and Jo gave him a cheeky grin. She let out a sudden terrible groan and slumped to the floor, holding the rail with her hands to conceal the opened handcuffs. Jo thrashed and moaned, and gave the most terrible gasps, until the alarmed guard came running across. 'The girl's collapsed,' shouted Stubbs. 'She was lost on Solos without a mask. You'd better get her one. The Marshal wants her alive, you know! You'll be for it if she dies.'

Fumbling for his oxy-mask, the guard leaned over Jo. While he tried to hold the mask to her face, she pulled her hands free, snatched the blaster from his belt, jumped up and backed away. 'Don't move,' she warned, and ran across to the desk and snatched up the key. Keeping him covered with the blaster, she freed the others one by one. Rubbing their wrists they looked at each other, wondering exactly what to do next. 'We've got to get a message to someone in authority,' said Jo, at last. 'We can't defeat the Marshal on our own.'

Cotton had an inspiration. 'We can tell the Investigator. His ship will be in range by now. The Marshal's desk communicator will be powerful enough!'

Stubbs took the blaster from Jo, shoved the still bemused guard to one side and locked the main door. 'All right, get on with it. I'll keep an eye out.'

Cotton fiddled with the transmitter, trying to find the right wavelength. 'Skybase One calling *Hyperion*. Urgent. Skybase One calling *Hyperion*. Urgent.' He repeated the message over and over again.

There was the sound of shouts and hammering from outside the door. 'Get a move on,' warned Stubbs. 'I shan't be able to hold them long once they're through.'

The doors burst suddenly open, and several guards fell into the room. They checked at the sight of the blaster steady in Stubbs' hand. 'All right, lads, stay right where you are. I don't want to shoot unless I have to.' Such was the authority in his voice that the guards obeyed. 'Now then, out you go and take your chum here with you.'

Hands raised, the guards backed meekly through the door.

Cotton's voice went on. 'Come in *Hyperion*. This is urgent. Skybase One on open channel.'

Blaster in hand, the Marshal suddenly appeared in the doorway, shouldering his way through the guards. 'Are you all frightened of one man? Get him!' The Marshal opened fire and Stubbs fired back, dropping behind the desk for cover. Jo and Ky dropped to the floor.

The Marshal and his guards jumped back, taking what cover they could in the corridor. Over the sizzling of blaster-bolts a voice crackled from the Marshal's transmitter. 'Skybase One, this is *Hyperion*.'

'We got 'em, Stubbsy,' shouted Cotton excitedly. Stubbs looked round, and a blaster bolt took him in the shoulder. He winced, but his voice was calm. 'Get on with it, then.' Ignoring the spreading pain, he went on firing at intervals through the doorway.

Cotton was suddenly embarrassed. 'Hey, what do I *say*?'

Jo ran to the communicator. 'Here, let me.' Rapidly she arranged her thoughts and started transmitting. 'Situation on Solos critical. Marshal's illegal atmosphere-conversion experiments causing severe loss of life. Administrator's recent assassination was at Marshal's direct orders. The Marshal is planning to seize permanent control of this planet. Please record and investigate this message. This is an emergency situation. No further transmission possible.'

There was a considerable pause while the *Hyperion* operator took in this staggering collection of information. A rather shaken voice came over the communicator. 'Message received and noted, Skybase One. Request identification, additional information soonest. *Hyperion* out.'

Stubbs was hit again, and the blaster fell from his hand. Ky dragged him clear of the doorway. Cotton snatched up the blaster and continued the covering fire through the doorway.

Without looking behind him, Cotton called, 'Stubbsy, you all right?'

Faintly Stubbs' voice came back. 'Did you get through?'

'Yes, we reached them ...'

'Good lad, Cotton,' said the faint voice approvingly. 'Good——'

Cotton turned round. Stubbs lolled back in Ky's arms, his head slumped. Cotton fired another blast, and wriggled back to him. 'Stubbsy? Come on, Stubbsy, mate ...' He looked in anguish at Ky, who shook his head.

Cotton's face was grim. 'We've got to get out of here.'

'How?' sobbed Jo.

'The Marshal's got a private exit—a hidden door behind his desk.' Cotton rushed to the wall and slid open a concealed panel beneath the mural.

Jo looked down at Stubbs. 'What about him?'

'Don't worry about him, miss,' said Cotton gently. 'He's all right. Now—move! The passage leads to the transfer system.'

Jo hesitated. She hated to leave the Doctor—but it was her presence that enabled the Marshal to blackmail him. Once they had escaped the Doctor would have a free hand.

Jo and Ky ran through the little door. With a final shot at the main entrance, Cotton followed, closing the panel behind him. Seconds later the Marshal and his guards rushed into the room.

Except for the body of Stubbs, the room was empty.

13

The Investigator

The Doctor was busily completing the control-mechanism that would divert the colossal power of the Skybase maser beam from the transfer area to Jaeger's laboratory.

With his usual ruthless efficiency, he had cannibalised most of Jaeger's equipment to rig up a ricketty-looking control console, festooned with trailing, many-coloured wires. He looked up from his work as distant sounds of shouting and blaster-fire reached the laboratory. 'What's that?'

Jaeger was busy at another section of the console. 'I've finished here, Doctor. Are you ready for me to isolate the transfer maser?'

'What? Oh, yes, yes, I am. Carry on!' The Doctor was still bothered by the shots, wondering if Jo and his friends were involved. But he knew the Marshal had posted armed guards outside the laboratory door. He went on with his work.

It took the Marshal only a moment to realise his quarry must have disappeared down his own private bolt-hole. Rushing to the panel he flung it open. 'Some of you come with me. The others make for the transfer system and cut them off!'

Jo, Ky and Cotton pelted down the corridor. The exit had been installed to enable the Marshal to come and go secretly between Skybase and Solos, and it looked like being their salvation. The corridor ended in another panel, which opened onto the corridor by the transfer booths. They heard footsteps following them, and others approaching ahead. But by now they were all piling into a transfer cubicle. Cotton stabbed frantically at the controls as the footsteps came nearer ... There was a hum of power as the booth began to activate ...

Jaeger looked up. 'Ready, Doctor?'

The Doctor studied his array of controls. 'Ready!' he confirmed.

Jaeger reached for the main power-switch. 'Transfer-system being isolated—now!'

He pulled the switch.

In the transfer cubicles the hum of power died away. Jo and the others stood in the cubicle, trapped. The Marshal and his guards ran up and surrounded them.

For a moment the Marshal himself was puzzled. Then he remembered Jaeger's urgent request of some time before and smiled. 'I'm afraid the transfer system is temporarily out of service, Miss Grant. A special request from your friend the Doctor.'

He waved the guards forward. One of them snatched the blaster from Cotton's hand. The Marshal called the guard Captain and said quietly, 'Take the traitor and the native to the thaesium radiation chamber. Say nothing to anyone about their whereabouts. Miss Grant, you come with me.'

Unaware that the first stage of his experiment had prevented the escape of his friends, the Doctor was carefully channelling the colossal power of the maser beam into a control-console that had never been meant to receive it, in order to use it for a purpose for which it had never been designed. With Jaeger watching on nervously, the Doctor was sliding a series of metal control-rods into the main power-core of the console. Just to cheer up his unwilling colleague, the

Doctor kept up a running commentary on the dangers of the operation as he worked. 'You do realise, Jaeger, that the slightest accident at this stage of the proceedings—whoops!' The Doctor nearly dropped a rod, caught it again, and went on with his work. Jaeger shuddered. 'As I was saying,' continued the Doctor cheerfully, 'an accident at this stage would reverse-transmit the whole of Skybase into anti-matter. We'd be blasted instantly to the other side of the universe, in a flash of electro-magnetic radiation. Fascinating thought that. We'd be un-persons, doing un-things, in an un-world ... un-together. Ah, got it.' The last power control rod slid safely home. The Doctor rose and stretched. 'In a minute or two we'll switch on and see what happens—or un-happens, as the case may be!'

Relieved of the tension of the experiment, the Doctor wandered round the laboratory, chatting amiably. 'I didn't tell you, did I? I ran into Professor Sondergaard, and I think we've discovered what's behind the mutations. It isn't a sickness at all ...'

Sondergaard ran into his greatest danger at what seemed the very moment of safety. Moving slowly and in easy stages he had reached the caves unseen. Not until he was in the galleries, close to his beloved laboratory, did he come across one of the Marshal's guards. The guard raised his blaster. The Captain's orders had been clear. No questions, no discussions, just shoot any survivors on sight.

Sondergaard looked at the guard's impassive face and gave himself up for lost. Then a massive shape scuttled out of the darkness and struck the man down. It was a Mutant, a huge insectoid creature in the final stages of the change.

Claws outstretched, it shuffled towards Sondergaard. Other Mutants came out of the darkness to join it, and soon he was surrounded.

He forced himself to stand his ground and remain calm. A wild plan was forming in Professor Sondergaard's mind. He had communicated with Mutants before, he could do so again. Perhaps he wasn't so powerless to help the Doctor after all.

Sondergaard began speaking in a low soothing voice. 'Listen, can you understand me? Can you? You saved me from the guard. Do you know who I am? I am Sondergaard. I help all the Mutants ... you remember.'

The Mutants checked their advance. They were listening!

Urgently Sondergaard asked, 'How many of you survived the gas attack, and the rockets?'

Incredibly the leading Mutant spoke. The hissing voice was barely intelligible. 'Many live ... but most sleep ... sick ...'

'No, not sick, we know that now. You are meant to change. But the Overlord's experiments with the atmosphere accelerated the Mutation rate, made the change happen wrongly. But that can be put right. The change can be made to go as it was meant to go ... But first you must help me find the Doctor. Will you come with me to Skybase?' Sondergaard put all the urgent persuasion he could into his final appeal. 'Will you come to find the Doctor—to save your people?'

The Doctor and Jaeger were hard at work on the second stage of the Doctor's plan to cure the spreading contagion of Solos.

They were both crouched over different sections of the huge improvised control console. 'Start the power build-up,' ordered the Doctor tensely.

Cautiously Jaeger touched the controls. 'Power running up to maximum—now!'

The Doctor's part of the console throbbed with

life. Beside the Doctor was an illuminated screen on which was projected a grid-plan of Solos. The Doctor checked the co-ordinates of the first contagion spot. 'Right, here we go—activate!' He threw a power switch and there was a rising hum of power. 'Hold the beam steady, man,' shouted the Doctor.

(Far below on Solos several square miles of already charred jungle burst into a holocaust of white-hot flame.)

The Doctor switched off the power and sat back mopping his brow. 'That's the first one. Now let's get on with the others.' Slowly the Doctor completed his delicate, dangerous task. One by one the contagion spots on Solos were blasted by the searing power of the boosted maser-beam, reducing whole areas to ashes—but killing the deadly infection they contained.

At last the Doctor sat back. 'There, that's the last one. What do your monitor readings show?'

Jaeger crossed to a complex panel of dials on the other side of the laboratory. 'The planet surface is completely free from contamination,' he said shakily.

'And the nitrogen isotope level?'

'Exactly as it was before I began my experiments.'

'Excellent. That's how it stays!'

'Not so, Doctor,' said a gloating voice. 'You will continue to co-operate with Professor Jaeger until you have given Solos an atmosphere breathable by humans—and only by humans!'

'I shall do no such thing,' said the Doctor indignantly.

'Very well.' The Marshal turned and shouted, 'Bring in Miss Grant.' A guard shoved Jo into the room, and the Marshal grabbed her by the wrist with one hand and drew his blaster with the other. 'Now then, Doctor ...'

The calm voice of the Skybase Computer made them all look up. 'Attention, attention. Investigator's ship *Hyperion* is about to dock!'

The Doctor smiled. 'It seems your superiors have

arrived, Marshal. What are you going to do now?'

The Marshal shoved Jo back into the arms of the guard. 'Put her with the others.' Jo was bundled away. 'Now, Doctor, we shall go and greet the Investigator —together!'

The radiation chamber was a bare metal room, distinguished only by a faint sinister glowing of the walls. A ladder leading to a hatch in the roof was the only way in and out. Jo gave the other two a rapid account of what had happened. 'As far as I can tell, this Investigator's arrived, and the Marshal and the Doctor have gone to meet him.'

Ky was slumped on the floor, looking very ill. He roused and looked up hopefully. 'Then my people can hope for justice?'

'I doubt it,' said Cotton laconically.

'Surely the Doctor will speak the truth?'

'With us down here as hostages?' Jo shook her head. 'We're here to make sure the Doctor says the right thing.' She leaned against the wall, but Cotton reached out and pulled her upright. 'Better stay away from that wall, miss. We're in the re-fuelling lock, next to where they store the active thaesium. That's why the walls glow.'

Jo backed away. 'Is it dangerous?'

'Not for a short time. Stay in here too long and— well, it builds up.'

'So how long will the Marshal keep us down here?'

Cotton shrugged. 'Who knows? Don't suppose he's too bothered about our health. Hey, wait a minute!' An expression of alarm spread over Cotton's face.

'What's the matter?'

'The Investigator's shuttle has just docked, right? And refuelling is automatic.'

Jo still didn't understand. 'What do you mean?'

'They'll be putting a probe through here any minute now, and the whole place will be flooded with live thaesium. Don't you see? The Marshal's arranged another of his little accidents!'

'He needs us alive,' protested Jo.

Cotton shook his head. 'He needs the Doctor to *think* we're alive, that's all.' He began pacing about, thinking hard. 'Once that probe comes through, we've got about thirty seconds before the place floods with live thaesium. But if we *use* that time ... Now listen carefully, both of you, there'll be no time for any mistakes.'

The Marshal and the Doctor stood waiting in the Marshal's office, the Doctor with amused patience, the Marshal in a state of seething rage. On arriving at the docking bay they had been greeted by the white-helmeted guards of Earth Council Security, and brusquely ordered to keep quiet and await instructions. All the Marshal's men were suspended and confined to their quarters, and the E.C.S. guards took over the base.

The Doctor had asked about his friends—but no one had been able to find them.

The Marshal marched up to the impassive E.C.S. guard at the door. 'I refuse to be treated like a ...' he spluttered, and stopped, for once at a loss for words.

'A criminal,' suggested the Doctor helpfully. The Marshal choked with rage.

The doors opened and the Investigator made a solemn entrance. He was tall and thin with a beaky-nosed aristocratic face. Beside him stood a younger aide, trying to look as much like his master as possible. 'My apologies for the delay, Marshal. I have been studying your log-book.'

The Marshal smiled. His log-book was kept very carefully indeed, and it showed events precisely as the Marshal wanted them to be shown.

The Investigator looked at the Doctor. 'And who is this gentleman?'

'I thought you already knew each other,' muttered the Marshal.

'Perhaps I should explain,' offered the Doctor.

The Investigator raised an impatient hand. 'All in good time. Now, Marshal, you may consider this a preliminary informal enquiry.' To the Marshal's rage, the Investigator settled himself behind *his* desk, in *his* chair, and looked up at him severely. 'You have been accused of some very serious crimes, Marshal. Well?'

Crushing his desire to yank the Investigator out of his chair and boot him out of the room, the Marshal forced his face into an ingratiating smile. 'Every colony commander is faced with this kind of accusation.'

'Only some. And sometimes the accusations prove to be true. That is why I am here ...'

'Of course you are,' said the Marshal, struggling to gather his wits. He launched upon a speech of defence. 'Solos has been beset by problems recently. After the assassination of the Administrator I decided to impose martial law. I took personal control of operations and tracked the terrorists to their hideout in the disused thacsium mines. I ordered the area cordoned off and the exits blown up.'

The Investigator frowned. 'Even though there were other Solonian natives inside—as well as the terrorists?'

'The other natives were all Mutts.'

The Investigator frowned. 'Mutts?'

The Marshal glared at the Doctor, who said reluctantly, 'The Marshal means that they were all plague victims. They used the caves as a refuge.'

'They were incurable,' said the Marshal sadly. 'I couldn't risk allowing the plague to spread.'

'This term "Mutts" ...'

'Mutant Natives,' explained the Doctor. 'A local expression for medically accelerated genetic metamorphosis.'

The Investigator said sharply, 'You are a scientist, I take it—a doctor?'

'Yes.'

'Qualified in?'

'Practically everything,' said the Doctor matter-of-factly.

'I see. Do you confirm the Marshal's diagnosis that these unfortunate natives were incurable?'

There was a tense pause. The Marshal gave the Doctor a meaning look—and the Doctor thought of his friends, hidden away somewhere, still prisoners in the Marshal's hands. He could appeal to the Investigator for help—but would he be believed?

'Well,' demanded the Investigator, 'were these natives incurable?'

The Doctor nodded. 'Yes,' he said slowly. 'I'm afraid they were.'

Although the Doctor didn't know it, his friends were now in deadly danger. Dwarfed by the enormous bulk of Skybase, *Hyperion* clung snugly to the arrival dock. A flexible probe appeared from the side of the ship. Guided by remote control it slid forwards to connect with the skybase fuel-bay.

There was a momentary pause in the Investigator's proceedings, while Jaeger was found. He sidled up to the Marshal. 'You realise *Hyperion* has started re-fuelling?'

'I suppose it must have.'

'Your prisoners are in the fuel lock,' hissed Jaeger. 'If they get caught in the thaesium stream ...'

'They will be totally destroyed.' The Marshal smiled. 'Convenient, isn't it?'

In the radiation chamber, Ky, Jo and Cotton heard an echoing clang. 'Here it comes,' whispered Cotton. 'Now remember—we've got thirty seconds!'

14

The Witnesses

Already the walls were glowing with increased brightness. 'Now sure you've got it straight, everybody? Any minute now the *Hyperion* probe will come through *there*.' Cotton indicated one wall. 'Then the relay tunnel will open on the other side—there.' He pointed again. 'We've got thirty seconds to get up the tunnel, through it and out of it again, before thaesium starts flooding through.'

With a startlingly loud click an iris-shaped opening appeared in one wall, admitting the open end of a long tube like an open-mouthed metal snake.

'There's the probe,' whispered Cotton. 'Now be ready! All right, Ky?' Pale and sweating, Ky nodded grimly. They were all poised like sprinters at the beginning of a race.

In the other wall a circular door slid back to reveal a narrow tube. As soon as the door was open, Cotton bundled Jo inside. He pushed Ky after her then scrambled up himself. They scrabbled their way up the smooth metal tube like rats in a drain pipe and emerged into a smaller version of the chamber they'd just left. Cotton began heaving on a bulkhead locking wheel. Jo and Ky helped him. The wheel turned, the bulkhead opened and they tumbled through. Instantly Cotton slammed the door behind them, spinning the wheel to close it fast. There was a roar on the other side of the door as the thaesium transfer got under way.

They stood for a moment, gasping with relief. Jo looked around. They were in an engineering area where complex machinery hummed quietly to itself.

'All automatic here,' whispered Cotton. 'That's

why there's no one about. Come on.' He led them away.

Professor Jaeger was answering the Investigator's probing questions, and making a very poor job of it. He was cringing and defiant by turns, and it was clear that he was making a very bad impression.

'Nevertheless, Professor,' the Investigator was saying, 'you *were* involved in experiments to change the planet's natural atmosphere?'

'Only in the laboratory, sir. It was all theoretical.'

'Then what of this charge that you actually attempted to make the air breathable by humans but not by Solonians? That these experiments were a cause of the outbreak of mutations?'

'Rubbish. All rubbish. I am a scientist ...' The Doctor coughed loudly and Jaeger glared at him. 'I am a scientist,' he repeated, 'and I rest my case on scientific grounds. Check the monitors—the atmosphere of Solos is what it has always been.'

'No thanks to you,' thought the Doctor indignantly. It had taken him a lot of hard and dangerous work to put Solos right again.

Cheered by having made this impressive point Jaeger went on, 'As for the Mutts—I beg your pardon, the Mutants, I did my best to find a cure—but it wasn't possible.'

There came the sound of shouting and scuffling from outside and to his joy the Doctor heard a familiar voice. 'Let me in. I've got to get in—it's vital.'

The Doctor rushed to the door, opened it before anyone could stop him, pulled Jo from the grip of a guard and dragged her inside. Ky and Cotton followed. His arm around Jo's shoulders, the Doctor stood before the astonished Investigator, who was seething with icy rage. 'What is happening here? Who are these people?'

The Doctor raised his voice commandingly. 'These,

Investigator, are missing witnesses. Miss Grant here is my assistant, kept hostage to ensure my unwilling co-operation in this travesty of justice.'

The Investigator tried to protest, but the Doctor gave him no chance. 'I must ask you to forget anything I may have said or implied up to now.' The Doctor pointed to the Marshal. 'I accuse *this* man ...' the accusing finger swung round to Jaeger '... and *this* man, of the most callous and brutal series of crimes against a defenceless race that it has ever been my experience to encounter.'

Sondergaard herded his unwilling party of Mutants along the transfer station corridor and up to the booths. He tried to persuade them inside, but they backed away hissing in fear. Sondergaard sighed in despair. With tremendous efforts he had persuaded a handful of Mutants to follow him across country, but now this final obstacle was proving too much for them. 'There is nothing to fear,' he urged. 'Look, I shall go in myself.' He stepped into a transfer booth and made a last appeal. 'I cannot help you until I find the Doctor. Will you come with me?'

The Mutants were backing away down the corridor. 'Very well,' said Sondergaard sadly, 'then I shall go alone. If I fail you will stay as you are—forever!' He operated the controls and vanished from their sight.

The Doctor concluded a speech of savage accusation. 'You hunted down and destroyed these poor creatures, Marshal, for no reason at all.'

The Marshal folded his arms defiantly. 'It was my duty to save the planet from contamination.'

'Your duty to save it for yourself!'

The Marshal lost his precarious hold on his temper. 'They were Mutts, do you hear me, Mutts!' he raged.

114

'Filthy diseased creatures. They must be wiped off the face of the planet!' His face was scarlet and he was almost mad with rage.

The Doctor looked coldly at him. 'Need I say more, Investigator?'

The Marshal saw the distaste in the Investigator's eyes, and realised that he had just condemned himself.

The Investigator was conferring in whispers with his advisers. He looked up. 'These scrolls you mention, Doctor. Could we see them?'

'Of course.' The Doctor reached in his pocket, then checked himself. 'I'm sorry, they're still with Professor Sondergaard.'

'And he is?'

The Doctor shrugged. 'I'm not sure. Presumably somewhere on Solos.'

'So you have no actual proof that these mutations are not harmful?'

The Marshal seized his advantage. 'He can prove nothing—*nothing*. It is all malicious lies.'

There was another interruption, the doors opened again and Sondergaard entered in the grip of a guard.

The Investigator sighed. 'Another missing witness, I presume?'

'This is Professor Sondergaard,' said the Doctor exultantly. 'He has lived and worked on Solos for many years. He can tell you what the Marshal has been doing.'

Sondergaard looked round baffled. 'What is happening here, Doctor?'

'Just a much needed investigation,' said the Doctor soothingly. 'Perhaps you'd be kind enough to tell the Investigator of our work in your laboratory?'

Sondergaard's face lit up at the sound of the only thing that really interested him ... the study of Solos and its mysteries. Automatically he fell into a lecture-room manner. 'Well, gentlemen, as I'm sure my colleague the Doctor has told you, we discovered that the mutations are not a disease, but a natural process which has somehow gone wrong.'

The Marshal jumped to his feet. 'I tell you the Mutts are evil. They should be destroyed!'

On Solos, the leader of Sondergaard's band of Mutants moved slowly into one of the cubicles. Sondergaard's words had reached some last vestige of understanding, and obscurely it felt a sense of duty. It stabbed with its claw at the controls, and more by luck than anything else, hit the transfer button. It materialised on Skybase, emerged, and began shambling down the corridor in search of Sondergaard ...

The Marshal had been restrained and Sondergaard was continuing his evidence. 'I beg you not to listen to the Marshal, sir! The Mutants are not monsters, they are the native life-form of Solos undergoing a natural and inevitable change ... This change however had been brought about prematurely by Jaeger's rash and callous experiments.'

'That is a lie,' shrieked Jaeger. 'Where is your proof?'

A tremendous hubbub broke out outside the door, quite different from the ones that had gone on before. Mixed in with shouts and screams was a high-pitched angry chittering noise. Sondergaard ran to the door and flung it open. The Mutant stood in the doorway. One of the guards raised his blaster, but Sondergaard struck it down. 'There is nothing to fear,' he shouted. 'The Mutants are not dangerous unless you try to harm them.'

'Look at it,' shouted the Marshal. 'It's vermin! It doesn't deserve to live.'

'It is a rational intelligent creature,' insisted Sondergaard. 'To kill it would be murder!'

The Marshal was looking hard at the Investigator.

He was backing away from the desk, his face full of fear and disgust. The Mutant stood swaying in the doorway, bemused by the crowd and the noise.

'Destroy it,' screamed the Marshal. 'Shoot it down, or we'll all be killed!'

A panic-stricken guard raised his blaster to obey. With amazing speed the Mutant slashed with a giant claw and the guard fell dying to the floor. The Marshal grabbed a blaster from the nearest guard and began pumping energy bolts into the Mutant's body. It fell back and back, staggering from the impact, until it collapsed in the doorway. The Marshal stood over it pumping charge after charge into the body until the blaster was finally exhausted. Panting, he strode over to the Investigator, who rose shakily from behind the desk. 'Now you see what I have to deal with. There may well be an army of those things awaiting to attack us down on Solos. Skybase may be swarming with them already. Investigator, if you value your own life you'll release my men—now—and place *your* men under *my* command.'

'You mustn't do that,' shouted the Doctor. But it was too late. All the Investigator's calm authority had vanished, shattered by the terrifying appearance of the Mutant and the brutality with which the Marshal had destroyed it. Perhaps such matters *were* best left to those with the experience to handle them, he thought. Contrasted with the danger of the Mutants, the Marshal's massive form seemed a shield rather than a menace.

Nervously, the Investigator turned to his aide. 'Release the Marshal's men, and instruct our own to obey his orders during the crisis.' He turned and hurried away to barricade himself in his quarters.

For a moment the Marshal was busy in the corridor, giving a string of orders to the aide. The Doctor knew there wasn't much time . . .

He slipped back into the office and beckoned to Jo, Cotton and Ky. Sondergaard came over to join them.

'We've got to get out of here,' whispered the Doctor.

Cotton pointed. 'We can use the Marshal's private door again.' He slid open the panel and Jo, the Doctor and Sondergaard went through.

Ky was about to follow, but staggered dizzily and Cotton went to help him. There was a shout of, 'Stop them,' from the door, and both were seized by guards.

The Marshal, armed and in command once more, came lumbering up. 'What happened?'

Jaeger had been watching the whole thing. 'The Doctor, Sondergaard and the girl got away through there. These two weren't quick enough.' He indicated Cotton and Ky, now held under guard.

The Marshal brooded. 'I've just put a guard on the transfer area, they won't escape that way. Now where else—the laboratory! After them.' The Marshal seized hold of his newly-released guard Captain, and indicated Cotton and Ky. 'Put them back in the radiation chamber!'

'Sir, you can't,' protested Cotton. 'This man's ill.' Ky was pale and shaking, only standing with Cotton's help. The Marshal ignored him and the guard Captain hurried Ky and Cotton away.

Jo and Sondergaard were shoving a heavy bench across the laboratory door. 'It's the best we can do, Doctor,' gasped Jo. 'It won't hold them long.'

The Doctor was studying the crystal he had found in the caves under Jaeger's crystallography machine. The crystal seemed to glow with a strange light. He looked up as Sondergaard came over to him. 'If I can analyse the structure, we may be able to formulate a serum.'

'That will take hours,' said Sondergaard.

There came a sudden angry hammering on the door. 'I don't think we've got hours,' said Jo warningly. 'Whatever you're doing, Doctor, you'd better get a move on!'

The Doctor nodded. 'I'll just have to try and accelerate the process.' He adjusted controls, the crystal glowed more fiercely and the Doctor looked up delightedly. 'Of course—we don't need a serum. The crystal itself will act as a bio-catalytic agent. It's a kind of emergency measure, left by the Old Ones for this very purpose!' He handed the crystal to Sondergaard. 'I think you'd better take this, Professor. You've got to get it to Ky.'

Sondergaard took the crystal. 'But surely the thaesium radiation is a vital part of the process?'

'There's thaesium radiation in the chamber where they put us,' said Jo. 'If he sends Ky back there and puts us in with him ...'

Sondergaard hid the crystal. 'It's a thin chance, Doctor ...'

'What else can we do? If we can only achieve a *successful* Mutation.' He was interrupted by the bursting open of the door and the arrival of the exultant Marshal, surrounded as usual by armed guards.

The Doctor gave him a cheery nod. 'Ah, there you are! Managed to wriggle your way out of trouble, have you?'

A happy smile spread over the Marshal's broad face. 'I am once more in full command of Skybase, Doctor. A fact you will do well to remember.' He summoned a guard. 'Put that old fool Sondergaard and the girl in with the other two.'

Jo and Sondergaard were marched out, and the Marshal and the Doctor looked at each other. The Doctor sighed. 'Well, what do you want?'

'Earth atmosphere for Solos, Doctor. No more, no less. Use particle reversal or any method you fancy— but *do* it. While you work, your friends will be confined in the radiation chamber. The thaesium level is a little high at the moment, so you'd better hurry, Doctor.'

*   *   *

Sondergaard looked up from his examination of Ky. 'How long has he been like this, Cotton?'

'Started the first time we were put in here. That didn't do him any good—and now this second dose ...'

Sondergaard took the glowing crystal from beneath his clothes. 'This is all I can do for him. We may already be too late ...' He handed the crystal to Ky, who clutched fiercely at it, hugging it to him. The glow of the crystal seemed to spread through Ky's whole body.

Sondergaard stepped back, watching carefully. 'Now what?' whispered Jo.

'We wait!'

Ky started moaning and thrashing about, hurling his body from side to side. 'He's getting worse,' cried Jo.

She went to help Ky but Sondergaard pulled her back. 'No, leave him!'

With amazing speed, Ky's body began changing. It was like looking at speeded-up film. His spine arched and grew great knobbly vertebrae. His head became that of a giant insect, his hands were suddenly fierce claws. Ky was turning into a Mutant before their eyes.

15

The Change

Watched by Jaeger and the Marshal, the Doctor was repairing his burnt-out particle reversal machine. 'Watch him like a hawk, it's about all you're good for,' snarled the Marshal.

The Doctor worked busily. The machine would soon become operational again—but it would never do what the Marshal hoped. Calmly, deliberately, the Doctor was converting it into a bomb, under the eye of his captor.

The Investigator came into the laboratory. When no more Mutants had appeared, he had recovered some of his old assurance. But he found things very different when he finally emerged from his quarters. 'Ah, there you are, Marshal,' he said peevishly. 'Why have my men been disarmed and confined to their quarters? What's all this about not allowing us to leave Skybase?'

The Marshal smiled blandly. 'I'm sure you and your men will enjoy your stay on Solos.'

'On Solos?'

'That's right. As soon as the good Doctor here has finished his twiddling, Solos will have a new atmosphere. You and your men will be the first settlers—on New Earth.'

The Doctor smiled ironically. 'And you, Marshal?'

'I shall rule from here on Skybase—just as I've always done.'

The Investigator could scarcely take in the Marshal's scheme. 'But more ships will come from Earth . . .'

'They will be welcome,' said the Marshal grandly. 'New Earth has room for all.'

The Doctor smiled at the almost comic dismay on

the Investigator's aristocratic face. 'Don't worry,' he said soothingly. 'He's quite mad, you know.'

The Marshal grinned savagely. 'No, Doctor, I told you. Madmen lose—and I have won. When will your work be finished?'

'Soon. What about my friends?'

'They will be released when the job is done—and not before.'

Jo, Sondergaard and Cotton watched in fascination as Ky's body went through the full range of Mutation —and beyond. The insect-like body of the Mutant straightened and became more humanoid, though this time it was taller and thinner than before. It glowed brighter and brighter, absorbing the thaesium radiation through the walls.

'What's happening now?' whispered Jo.

Sondergaard shook his head. 'I don't know, my child. We can only watch—and hope.'

There was a final flare of radiation, and Ky's body seemed to rise and float to the top of the steps. Jo and the others looked up in amazement at the strange creature into which Ky had evolved ... a slender glowing figure bathed in light, with a calm and beautiful face (although Jo didn't know it, the Doctor had seen just such a face in the globe on the glowing cave. It was the face of the Old Ones, the highest form of Solonian life).

'It worked,' breathed Sondergaard reverently. 'Thank heavens, it worked!'

Nervously Jo called, 'Ky, can you hear me?'

The figure did not open its mouth, but each one of them heard the calm, beautiful voice inside their heads. 'I hear you,' it said.

'Thought transference,' murmured Sondergaard. 'Wonderful.'

Cotton, although considerably impressed, had a

more practical turn of mind. 'It's marvellous all right. But can he get us out?'

Jo called, 'Ky, can you help us?'

'There is little I cannot do—now,' said the voice. 'Ky thanks you. You have saved my people. You have shown me the way ...'

The glowing figure faded *through* the metal wall and disappeared.

'That's great,' said Cotton disgustedly. 'Just flashes off, and leaves us here.'

As if in answer to Cotton's reproof, the door to the chamber flew silently open. 'That's more like it,' said Cotton cheerfully. 'Come on, everyone, out we go.'

The being that had once been Ky *floated* along the corridors of Skybase leaving a trail of radiance. Two astonished guards tried to stop it, and were casually flung back by some immense unseen force. The figure floated on.

The Doctor straightened up and surveyed the now-repaired particle reversal apparatus. 'Are you ready?' asked the Marshal impatiently.

The Doctor nodded. 'Ready for an initial test. You don't do this sort of thing in a flash, you know.' He reached for the switch. 'You know that if your scheme does work, you'll destroy a life-form unique in the universe?'

'Just get on with it, Doctor.'

The Doctor bowed his head. 'As you wish ...' He reached for the switch. 'Wait,' ordered the Marshal. 'I still don't trust you, Doctor. Jaeger—you operate it.'

The Doctor tried to conceal his feelings of relief as he moved away from the machine. In its present state, he thought it was a very good idea for someone else to switch on.

Jaeger threw the switch, and the strange-looking machine hummed with power. The noise rose higher and higher until it was almost a shriek, and the machine began to judder alarmingly.

'Something's gone wrong,' yelled the Marshal. 'Switch the thing off!'

Jaeger flicked frantically at the controls. Nothing happened. The noise rose higher, the juddering increased. 'I can't stop it,' screamed Jaeger. 'He's destroyed the safety circuits. It's going to overload!'

The Doctor swept the Investigator to the floor. 'Keep down,' he yelled. There was a shattering explosion and the machine blew up, killing Jaeger instantly, and blasting the Marshal off his feet. The Doctor helped the shaken Investigator to rise.

The laboratory was filled with smoke. As it cleared they could see that the particle reversal machine was totally and utterly wrecked. This was no case of a blown-out circuit. The machine was completely destroyed—just as the Doctor had planned. Most of the surrounding weather-control equipment was ruined too. There was no longer the slightest chance that this laboratory could be used to change the atmosphere on Solos—certainly not by Jaeger, who lay dead in the middle of the wreckage.

The Marshal had clambered to his feet. The blaster in his hand was trained unswervingly on the Doctor. 'You have destroyed my dreams, Doctor,' he said in a strangely calm voice. 'Now I shall destroy you.'

The Doctor waited calmly. He had not expected to survive his last desperate move. He had only wanted to make sure that Solos stayed as it was. If only his friends had managed to succeed with Ky ...

There was a sudden radiance in the doorway, and Ky materialised, glowing with unearthly light. He pointed a finger, and the blaster spun through the air. The Marshal stared stupidly down at his empty hand. He looked up in terror at the glowing figure.

He heard, as they all did, a voice inside his head. 'Die, Marshal. Let there be an end to your torture of my people.'

The Doctor and the others saw the Ky figure stretch out a hand towards the Marshal. They saw a beam of light blaze between the pointing hand and the Marshal's body. They saw the Marshal's massive bulk glow brighter, brighter—and blaze into nothingness. The glow faded and the Marshal was gone—forever.

The Doctor heard a voice inside his head. 'Ky thanks you, Doctor.' The glowing figure vanished.

Much, much later, they were all in the Marshal's office, trying to explain things to the Investigator, who was back behind the desk and rapidly recovering his self-assurance.

'All the other mutations were premature, you see,' explained the Doctor, 'triggered off too soon ... like butterflies that hatch on a warm winter day.'

The Investigator wondered how he was going to explain all this to Earth Council. 'But now you can remedy this?'

'Professor Sondergaard has agreed to stay on Solos, to see as many of the Solonians as possible through to the final stage of Mutation.'

Sondergaard nodded eagerly. 'Ky is on Solos now, with the crystal. Together we can save them.'

As the explanation went on, Jo whispered to Cotton. 'What will you do now?'

'Stay on and help to clear up the mess the Marshal made. Then we'll all do what we should have done long ago—go home. Back to Earth!'

The Investigator caught the end of this remark. 'Exactly so, Cotton. Meanwhile you will assume acting command of this base, pending its eventual return to Earth.' He turned to the Doctor and Jo. 'You two will return to Earth in *Hyperion* with me. There's still got to be a full enquiry of course—and I confess

I'm not entirely clear about your exact involvement in this affair.'

The Doctor rubbed his chin. 'Yes, yes, of course, Investigator. Anything you say. Meanwhile I wonder if you'll excuse us just for a moment. My assistant is feeling a little faint.'

Jo looked up innocently. 'No, honestly, I'm fine now Doctor . . . oof!' She gasped as a bony elbow caught her in the ribs.

The Doctor took her firmly by the arm. 'Dear me, Jo, I'm afraid you look quite ill. I think you've been overdoing it!'

He hustled Jo out of the room, ignoring her protests, and a few moments later they were running through the corridors of Skybase. At last the Doctor came to a halt. 'There we are!'

'Where?' gasped Jo.

'The storage area where we left the TARDIS.'

The Doctor touched the door-control. 'Oh no, they've repaired it and locked it again.' He took out his sonic screwdriver, and got to work.

Jo grinned. 'More breaking and entering, Doctor?' She remembered how worried she'd been at the Doctor's casual breaking open of doors when they'd first arrived. But rather a lot had happened since then.

The Doctor smiled. 'All in a good cause!' he said cheerfully.

The door slid back, revealing the little store-room in which they'd first arrived. The TARDIS was standing reassuringly in the corner. The Doctor opened the door.

Jo took a last look round. 'So we end up back where we started—in the broom cupboard!'

The Doctor chuckled. 'Yes . . . still, we made a pretty clean sweep of this place in the end!'

Jo groaned at the terrible joke. The Doctor ushered her inside the TARDIS and closed the door behind them. A few minutes later there was a wheezing, groaning sound and the police box faded away.

For a moment there was silence. Then the computer voice of the Skybase computer said reproachfully, 'Attention. Attention! Computer confirms door malfunction in Storage Area Three. Security to investigate please.'

Conscientious in his new duties, Acting-Marshal Cotton sent a couple of guards to check up. But by the time they arrived, Jo and the Doctor were far, far away ...